To Anna,

Hope you enjoy
the story — and your
school days at St. Annes!

Susan Beach

The Short and Tall Tales of Penelope

Magical Adventures in Germany

Written by Susan Beach

authorHOUSE®

AuthorHouse™
1663 Liberty Drive, Suite 200
Bloomington, IN 47403
www.authorhouse.com
Phone: 1-800-839-8640

First published by AuthorHouse 9/24/2009

ISBN: 978-1-4389-6367-9 (sc)

Illustrated by Stephanie Beach.

Printed in the United States of America
Bloomington, Indiana

This book is printed on acid-free paper.

Always and forever, this book is dedicated to my family, especially my three children, Ali, Amanda and Tyler who play no small part in this tale. Our adventure in Germany was nearly as fantastic as the one you are about to set upon.

Contents

The Strange Welcome

"...and please put your seats and tray tables in an up right position. *Vielen Dank, dass Sie mit Lufthansa geflogen sind.*"[1]

Penelope was suddenly jolted forward as her mom adjusted her seat for landing. Still mesmerized by thoughts of leaving home forever, she rubbed her eyes and reluctantly pulled her gaze away from the window. She turned to see four pairs of eyes focused on her.

"Penelope, what does Germany look like? Can you tell?" chimed her mom and dad together.

"I can't see anything! It's no fair she gets the window!" yelled Amelia.

"Um, all I can see is bunches of tiny white houses with orange roofs. The grass looks really green. I see a lot of hills and patches of dark trees. Lots of farms and stuff, I guess. Does it always rain like this, Dad? I hate rain," she said with a sigh as she twisted her long reddish blond hair around her finger. "Are we taking a train to the new house?"

"Train, train, on a train" her brother Tucker began to chant. "A fast train and go lemon speed!"

---

[1] Thank you for flying with Lufthansa

"You mean lightning speed, dummy" corrected Amelia with a know-it-all expression and rolled her eyes at Penelope. "I'm so glad I'm not a baby like him!" She shrugged her shoulders and shook out her super thick curly dark hair.

"Let's be nice. Remember he's only four honey", cautioned Mrs. Pond, her mother. "You and Penelope are the big sisters and must help your little brother. I know you're all tired from this long flight, but…"

Her dad interrupted, "you'll wake up when you see the big backyard, kids. There's even a fishpond. I know you're going to love our new house."

Penelope sat back against the airline seat and frowned, "I know I am gonna hate it here," she mumbled to herself.

In the airport arrivals area Penelope looked around at the new surroundings. It looked a lot like Washington DC's Dulles airport, only the signs were funny and the words made no sense.

"Dad, what does *Herzlich Willkommen*[2] mean? I keep seeing it everywhere," she questioned.

"It means hearty welcome because the Germans are happy you're here, honey," answered her mom. "Now where do you suppose we pick up Sammy?"

"Sammy!" the children cried in unison. Sammy, the family cat, had also flown on the jumbo jet, but had to travel in the cargo hold because the family was not sure he could remain quiet for the seven hour flight across the Atlantic.

"He's probably howling in the baggage area," joked Mr. Pond.

---

[2] Heartfelt Welcome

As the family made its way through the steady stream of travelers, Penelope kept checking out her new surroundings. She stared at all the busy, rushing people, dressed mostly in black. The air carried an unpleasant taste.

"I can't believe they allow smoking in the airport, Ben."

"Yeah, it looks like a forest fire in here," coughed Amelia dramatically. "And why," she added, "does everyone talk like they are clearing their throats? It sounds kinda' scary, I think."

"Some hearty welcome this is," agreed Penelope lugging her now even heavier backpack. "At least I won't be the tallest person in Germany", she surmised as she looked around.

Tall men and tall women hurried past with briefcases swinging; groups of tired-looking people shuffled along with bulging bags. Now and then Penelope would make contact with someone's eyes. But, in a wink, the eyes would disappear. At first this appeared to be a funny coincidence, but after a third time, she began to feel uneasy. Are they looking at *me*?" she wondered. She turned to her sister, "Amelia, do you keep seeing those eyes? I feel like I'm being watched."

"What? What eyes? What are you talking about?"

Penelope shook her head "Forget it. I must be imagining it," she muttered as she twisted and untwisted a strand of hair. Shrugging her slender shoulders, she followed her family through Customs and Immigration where they all had their passports stamped. The official in the booth, dressed in a green army-like uniform, smiled at Penelope as he handed back her passport.

"Such a tall young lady for ten years of age. *Willkommen nach Deutschland,*"[3] he nodded.

She answered thank you with the German *Danke*[4] and concluded it was the fact that she was five feet tall, practically a skyscraper, for a fourth grader, that made people stare.

After some confusion in locating a bathroom for a jumpy Tucker, who would practically run in place signaling his need to…go, they arrived in the baggage claim hall.

"Dad, look at these crazy baggage carts," Penelope noted as she attempted to steer it toward her dad. It kept moving in a circle. "All the wheels move at once. I can't control it. Ours are much better," she decided. Then she remembered Sammy. Penelope scanned the large room for Sammy and his cage. She spied the large kennel and started to tell her family when she noticed that something furry was OUTSIDE the kennel.

"What in the world is that?" she wondered and squeezed her wide spaced hazel eyes for a clearer picture.

It was definitely not a dog because it stood on two legs and was at least three feet tall. Even weirder, it was wearing what looked like a ballerina's dance costume.

"Mom, look! Over there!" she barely managed to get the words out. "It's a…a creature?" she stammered as she pointed.

"Oh good, you found him. Look everyone," her mom announced, "Penelope found Sammy."

The entire family ran over to the kennel. Except Penelope. Shaking her head, as if to clear cobwebs, she shuffled slowly after them. Was she still dreaming? Don't they see it? Ohmagosh!

---

[3] Welcome to Germany
[4] Thank you

The creature was winking. At HER. And it was smiling and wearing something pink. Suddenly it darted behind a suitcase so she yelled out loud, "Wait! Don't scare it away!"

She ran over, skidding into her mom and little brother. It was obvious that her family did not see the creature-person. They were looking at Sammy, the family cat. All of a sudden, the creature-person was no longer there as she approached the kennel.

"He keeps dropping his head down, Mom. What's wrong with him?" whimpered seven year old Amelia, as her large liquid chocolate eyes, so much darker than Penelope's, peered into the kennel.

Penelope took one look at her fat, furry friend, frightened and curled into a tight ball in the far corner of his kennel, and all thoughts of the strange creature she had spied earlier were immediately forgotten.

"Oh, let me hold him!" Penelope begged as she was reunited with her favorite cat. "He's just waking up, that's all" she cooed. She and her brother and sister took turns consoling and cajoling their sweet-tempered, but scared Sammy.

An hour later, as they sped along the wide *Autobahn*[5] toward their new home, her mom sighed, "Isn't the scenery pretty kids? It looks just like a fairytale land with all these dark tall forests. No wonder so many magical stories were written in Germany. The brothers Grimm lived north of here. You know, they wrote Hansel and Gretel and Rapunzel?"[6]

Penelope tried to keep her eyes open as she gazed through the rain-streaked window. She saw indeed lots of tall green

---

[5] Freeway
[6] Both Hansel and Gretel and Rapunzel are stories written down by the Brothers Grimm

trees and small clusters of white houses with brown stripes.[7] "Bet it isn't raining back at home!" she whispered as her stomach gave a low rumble. She felt a little sick to her stomach too, especially when she thought of her house and best friend Allyson in Annapolis. She's probably playing dolls in our tree house right now. Why did Daddy have to take this new job building a giant airship? All her tears and Amelia's too, hadn't changed her parents' minds. She could hear them over and over again: A big adventure! A chance to live abroad! Couldn't they see she didn't want a new adventure and she especially didn't want to move clear across the ocean to Europe? She had just recently memorized the fifty states. Her new school couldn't possibly be as fun as St. Anne's of Annapolis where she felt at home and had many friends.

Now here she was in rainy Germany, sitting on a cold car seat speeding toward a new life she didn't even want. She stared out the window feeling sorry for herself, not really seeing the beautiful, rolling countryside and low green hills. Then, all of a sudden a quick movement in the trees caught her eye.

"Look! What's that?" she shouted loudly, startling her tired family.

"What! Where? What is it?" They all cried in surprise.

"Back there, in the tree near the road. Oh wow, he's waving to me! He's so cute and little. He looks like a dwarf from <u>Snow White and the Seven Dwarves</u>![8] Cool! Ouch!" she cried seconds later as she bumped her head on the car's ceiling.

"Penelope, calm down. You don't want your father to crash this car. We are driving so fast. Ben, what *is* the speed limit

---

[7] *Fachwerk* Houses or Half-timbered houses (similar in style to Tudor)
[8] Another story from the Grimm collection.

here anyway?" She turned back to Penelope, "Perhaps it was a hedgehog you saw, or a baby deer? Maybe it was *Hansel*?" she winked.

"Mo-om! Stop joking. I saw a real live elf or dwarf or something like that, like in the storybooks. He was wearing a brown coat a...and…and matching brown pants!" she blurted out as she furiously twisted her hair around her fingers.

"I didn't get to see the eh…elf!" sobbed Amelia, fists clenched in frustration. "Turn around Daddy!"

"I saw IT!" yelled Tucker with a big grin. Nobody paid him any attention.

"Penelope, you must be special. The Germans even put out their fairytale characters for you," her dad said with an even bigger grin on his face. "We'll be at our house in a German minute because there is no speed limit on this section of the *Autobahn*. Let's go see if our new home has any mysterious creatures in it."

"I hope so!" grumbled Amelia as she frowned with her arms tightly crossed. Suddenly, a speeding object zoomed past the family car. The blur turned out to be a sleek *BMW*.[9]

"Whoa! He must be going almost 200 miles per hour!" Mr. Pond exclaimed with a touch of admiration in his voice.

Tucker grinned in his car seat, "Let's go lemon-speed Daddy!"

Mrs. Pond answered, "Let's not! I want to reach our home in one piece, Ben." She glared at her husband.

Penelope sat back against the seat and let out a huge sigh. She couldn't forget what she saw. "Wow," she muttered

---

[9] BMW a car made by Bavarian Motor Works, originally an airplane manufacturer, known for the propeller as its trademark logo.

to herself. "I know I'm not dreaming." She turned her head once more to the scenery outside, hoping to catch another glimpse of the little man-like creature. But only tall pines and gray houses sped by in a blur, accompanied by, now and then, a tall narrow church steeple. Hmmm, this place might not be so bad after all, she concluded. Her face brightened with a new thought, maybe the kids here will be tall like me and so they won't make fun of my height. Her so-called 'growth-spurt' was getting on her nerves. When she 'shot up like a flagpole' as her Dad liked to say, at the end of third grade year, she went from feeling normal and fitting in, to becoming the object of jokes and pointing snickering fingers.

They turned off the autobahn at a sign marked *Ausfahrt.*[10]

"Is *owsfort* our town, Dad? 'Cause I saw a lot of signs that say it. It must be a huge town," she decided.

"That's a good one", laughed her Dad explaining. "Actually honey, *Ausfahrt* means EXIT for the highway. You'll see a lot of those signs," he winked. Our town is called *Eppstein*[11]. The car slowed and snaked around some tight turns and very narrow roads. Up on a hill sat a castle in ruin.

"Wow, look at that castle. How romantic." Mrs. Pond pointed out, "It must be at least three hundred years old. We'll have to go and explore it." She nodded enthusiastically at the three skeptical faces of the children.

"Is that our house?" Amelia asked with raised brows that folded again into a big frown.

"No, no, of course not sweetie." Our house is much more modern."

---

[10] Exit
[11] Eppstein im Taunus, town NW of Frankfurt

"Is it 'fawling' down?" piped in Tucker in a serious voice.

"You can see for yourself, T-Boy, my son, because here we are." Mr. Pond maneuvered the car slowly down a long street with neat, square houses on each side. Everything appeared clean and orderly. "Check out the backyard," he bellowed as he pulled into the short but steep driveway. He turned to his wife Janet, "I think this move is going to be really good for our family. How often can you have a chance like this to experience another culture, live in a beautiful place with mountains and trees and castles?" he gestured with his arm. "And I can commute by train to *Frankfurt*[12]," he added.

"Yes, but Dad, you're not leaving your best friend and your school and your tree-house and your room and…" Penelope started to wind up and stifled a sob. Her mom smiled at her,

"I know it's hard to move away honey. You are very brave. But try to give Germany a chance. I promise you'll make new friends.

"Is this *Frankfoot*?" asked wide-eyed Tucker, as all five crowded through the front door at one time.

"It's *Frankfoort*, you dummy!" corrected Amelia. "And this is not *Frankfoort* silly. It's our house."

Penelope looked up and around. The house was similar to the ones they had passed on the highway. It was white with large wooden beams criss-crossing through it. She and her sister and brother raced around exploring all rooms, basement to attic. Then she remembered Sammy.

"Come on Sammy! There are no monsters here. Be a brave cat for once!" she gently scolded him as she coaxed him from his travel kennel. The three children followed Sammy around as

---

[12] Frankfurt, a major business center, is located in central Germany

he slinked and sniffed his way through each room and window ledge. The house was roomy and somewhat cavernous, bare wood floors stretched across large almost empty rooms. The kitchen was entirely white, white tile floors, white appliances, white walls and countertops. The house came 'furnished', though it contained only the bare essential furniture, a couch, a table and chairs and a picture of *Neuschwanstein*[13], the white castle with tall spires seen on puzzles and postcards everywhere, hung on the living room wall.

Penelope stopped and turned to her mom, who was busy inspecting the white kitchen. "The Germans really like things neat and tidy and well…white. Every wall is white. Can I paint my room orange?" she asked and twirled a piece of hair. "I think Sammy likes it here." Penelope picked the cat up in a great big hug. "Let's go play in my white room."

She climbed the wooden spiral staircase and entered the larger of the two bedrooms upstairs. She admired the tall, sloping ceilings and view outside onto the street. In the distance green-covered mountains completed the panoramic view. Penelope flopped down on the fluffy (yes, white) down-comforter on her wide adult-sized bed. The quaint room and soft bedding reminded her of <u>Heidi</u>[14], the story of the girl in the Alps, somehow.

"I wonder what the kids are like here?" she sighed aloud as she stroked Sammy's soft gray and white fur. Then her eyes widened as she remembered the creature. She peered across her room to the pair of large square windows. A tall green tree filled the glass. The mountain view was blocked by the pine

---

[13] Built by King Ludwig, a castle located in the Bavarian Alps
[14] <u>Heidi</u>, book by Johanna Spyri

needles. "Guess I'll find out at the International School next week," she hummed to herself and absent-mindedly twisted a strand of hair around her finger. All the classes at the new school were taught in English her parents promised. And there would be lots of kids like her who were new to Germany, and they too came from countries far away. Maybe even Maryland, USA. Someone at the new school would have to know about these strange creatures, she supposed.

Later that afternoon, as she and Sammy were about to doze off, Sammy gave a low growl and his hair fluffed out like a porcupine. Penelope sat up.

"What is it Sammy?" She followed his glare out the window to the tree, a tall pine that towered over the front of the house. She sprang to the sill and scanned the eye-level branches. "Is it the creature Sammy? I bet you saw one like I did. Don't be scared. He looked friendly. I think?" she muttered as she twisted several strands of her hair.

Suddenly the branches parted and out darted a small reddish squirrel with very pointy ears which then leapt onto the next branch in a flurry of motion. Sammy practically jumped through the glass to attack, but Penelope stopped him with her pealing laughter.

"Sammy, you tricked me!" She reached over to pick him up and cuddle him when her eyes spied a new movement. Something larger was in the tree, hurriedly scrambling down the levels of limbs.

"Ohmagosh!" she gasped through her fingers. "It's the creature from the car ride!" Before she could turn the lever to open the window, it was too late. The mysterious visitor had disappeared.

She ran downstairs. "MOMMY! DADDY! Amelia! Everyone! I saw another thing- man, whatever. He was just like the other creature I saw, but he was wearing green. I think. MOM!"

Out of breath, she found her family in the backyard looking at the fishpond. "Didn't you hear me?" she panted. "I saw another creature."

"Where? No fair! I wanna see one, too. She always gets to see everything!" scowled Amelia.

"Penelope dear, weren't you sleeping? It was so quiet upstairs," soothed her mom.

"Mom, I saw another little man-elf-creature. I swear. He was in the tree outside our window, in front of the house." She saw her mom give her dad the raised eyebrow look, which meant it was hopeless. They didn't believe her.

"Well, I think we have seen enough for one day," added her dad, giving her mom a knowing nod. "Let's grab a bite to eat and go to bed. Tomorrow, everything will make more sense." He motioned to the heavy glass door leading into the kitchen. "Look kiddo, at these German doors. They're magic. They open outward like a door," he demonstrated proudly, "and they also open like a window." He pushed the door at the top and it opened at an angle to allow air in and out. "What a great design. That should cheer you up," he chuckled.

"Yes, it has been a long day," agreed her mom, trying to sound cheerful. "I'm glad we're here safe and sound." She hugged Penelope and gently brushed some wayward strands of long hair from Penelope's still flushed face. "Let's get you to sleep. Then you can dream some more about these little magic creatures." She smiled and hugged Penelope even tighter.

Penelope, using her keen fourth grade mind, realized her parents would not believe her on her word alone. Somehow she had to prove she wasn't seeing things. The little creature was real. She knew it. And it wasn't that little. Tucked in her new bed cozy and warm, under the eaves with a goose down comforter, she was nearly asleep when she felt an eerie movement - the patter of little feet. Once more she bolted up, eyes wide with expectation, only to find Tucker at her bedside gazing down at her with large, limpid almost black eyes. He slipped his small hand into hers and whispered,

"Peppy? Did the other magic 'cweeture' have a furry face too?"

Penelope blinked twice, stared hard at her little brother and then smiled a wide smile. "You know, Tucker, he did have a beard as well! Let's show Mommy and Daddy there REALLY ARE fairy tales in Germany!" She hugged him and sent him padding down the hall back to his room. She curled up like a contented cat and fell asleep.

Helping Hand

"Mo-om, I'm home!" yelled Penelope out of breath. She had run home from the bus stop. "No homework this weekend 'cause Mrs. Franchett was sick today. I'm going down to the post office for some candy, okay? I finished all the goodies in my *Schultüte*[15]. I love THAT German tradition!" She grinned as she was about to run back out the ground level cellar door.

"Penelope gets candy, so do I? I'm going too, Mom!" piped in Amelia as she and Tucker bumped into Penelope in the doorway. "Can I have some money or what-ever-you-call-it, umm E*uros*?[16] Her loud voice was cut short as she saw the stern look on her mom's face as she came down the stairs.

"Girls, not so loud. It is still *Ruhezeit*[17]," she whispered, pointing towards the neighbors.

"Oh Mom, quiet time ends at three o'clock." Penelope rolled her eyes. "Germany sure has weird rules. Why can't there be noise in the afternoon?"

"Well, I'm sure it has something to do with community peace and quiet. After all, babies nap in the afternoon and…

---

[15] A cone shaped bag filled with candy and school supplies, traditionally given to students on the first day of school

[16] Euros are the currency in Europe. Germany is part of the European Union

[17] Quiet Time is typically from 1:00pm until 3:00pm

14

anyway, please mail this letter to Grandma. Oh, and don't forget to bring back something for your little brother," Mrs. Pond winked to Tucker. "Someday, when he's a bit bigger, he can come with you."

Ponytails flowing behind them, Penelope and Amelia skipped down the hill toward the village center. The streets became smaller and narrower as they approached the oldest part of town or as the Germans called it, the *Altstadt*.[18] They passed the butcher, *Metzgerei Haller*[19] where plates of red meat, mostly pork, gleamed in the shiny clean windows. The *Bäckerei*[20] beckoned with displays of whipped-cream and chocolate-topped *Torten*[21] and *Kuchen*[22]; cakes that looked so delicious they looked like they belonged in a fairy-tale. The girls didn't give these delicious goodies a second look. Their favorite candies and sweets awaited them at the multi-purpose post office.

"I think you and Tucker are tricking us all," panted Amelia on the way there as she sought to keep pace with her sister, always trying to close the two year age gap. "You never saw something like an elf or dwarf, or any creature. You wanna make us believe you did. Elves are just pretend anyway. Daddy told me."

"Amelia, I am not lying!! No one believes me. Not one person in my class. The mean boys even call me 'Penelope-make-believe.' How do you think that makes me feel?!"

---

[18] Old or ancient part of a town or city
[19] Haller's Butcher Shop
[20] Bakery
[21] Fancy cakes and pies
[22] cakes

What she did not admit to her sister was that they also called her *'gross girl'*[23] because she was so much taller than the other kids. *Gross* meant 'big' in German. It was so embarrassing and it hurt her feelings a lot, but she quickly forgot her height as she entered *Der Roll Laden*[24], which was the name of the post office.

The 'post office' was really a store where one could mail a package, pick up dry-cleaning, pay a telephone bill, buy school supplies, toys, magazines and, of course, candy. One could even buy shutters for a house, because *Rolladen* was named for the room-darkening blinds that most German homes used on their windows. There was nothing like it back at 'home' in the states. The shop was only the size of a small bedroom but every corner and cranny had a purpose.

Penelope thought to herself: "Besides, I'll probably never see another elf - whatever - again anyway," she sighed as she looked over the candy selection.

She was beginning to doubt her own memory since it had been a month since she had seen him, or it (she was sure it was a he anyway). Every morning on the bus ride to and from school she scanned the countryside looking for a quick movement or simply a sign of some sort. Once at school she thought she had seen a strange short and chubby figure, but it turned out to be a cardboard snowman made by the kindergartners. Unfortunately she realized this fact too late. She had started talking to it, before seeing what it really was. A group of sixth graders had seen her and they immediately

---

[23] Big girl
[24] Shutters

started laughing and pointing at her. Hiding tears, she had wanted to run away on one of the fast German trains.

"Maybe they'll finish that new train track near our house and I can sneak away on it one day," she reasoned feeling quite sorry for herself. One glance at her sister snapped her out of her self-pity. "Amelia, not another extra *sauer gummi*![25] You are so greedy!"

Amelia handed the owner of *Der Roll Laden*, the woman the girls referred to as 'the post lady', the letter to be stamped and un-cupped her hand full of sticky gummis, spilling the tiny bears all over the counter. Embarrassed, Penelope too, added her goodies to the pile.

"*Macht nichts,*"[26] whispered the post lady with a wave of her brown spotted hand. Slowly, she counted the candies and gave Amelia some change. She turned and looked up at Penelope and said with a half smile, "*So, wie heisst Du, Liebschen?*"[27]

Penelope answered automatically "*Ich heisse Penelope.*"[28] She recognized immediately the German greeting she had been taught the first day in school. "My name is Penelope."

The post lady introduced herself as *Hexe*.[29] Penelope thought she looked sinister. Her hair was very straight and short like a boy's. Jet black, with bright blue strands around her face, it contrasted greatly with her pale skin. Although she smiled when she spoke to Penelope in German about Penelope's American family, her eyes had no twinkle and they bore like black icicles into Penelope's. Penelope translated a few friendly words with

---

[25] Sour Gummy Bear
[26] It's nothing (not to worry)
[27] What is your name honey?
[28] My name is Penelope
[29] Witch

her limited German vocabulary. She stood at attention when she heard Hexe say *"Schönen Tag noch,"*[30] for she knew the reply to 'Have a nice day'. "She answered cheerfully *"Danke gleichfalls, Auf Wiedersehen!"* [31]

Once outside, Amelia glared at Penelope with half open eyes and crossed arms. "What were you saying about me to the post lady?"

"Amelia, I didn't say anything about you. She was saying something about our family, I think. And then thank you and goodbye. She said to have a nice day. She always says that."

"Well, I think she is a mean old witch! She looks like one with that big crooked nose and squinty eyes!"

"You're just jealous you can't speak German!" Penelope rolled her eyes and headed up the hill toward home. "Mom said we are going on a long walk this weekend to explore the woods around the town. Maybe we'll see some horses," she added as an afterthought. Both she and her sister were crazy about horses and had even started lessons at a nearby stable.

"Maybe we'll see lit-tle mag-ic-al crea-tures?" taunted Amelia stretching out the words to annoy her sister as she tagged Penelope on the shoulder. "Hope you don't mind that I told my whole class that you believe in weird creatures, and always make up stories. Even my new friend, Lexi from Holland, thinks you're strange and she can't even speak English yet. Hey, last one home is a rotten *Ei!*[32] See, I know German, silly," she laughed.

The girls raced home with a gloating Amelia in the lead. Penelope slowed down to pop a chocolate into her mouth, tired

---

[30] Have a nice day
[31] Thank you, same to you. Till we see you again
[32] egg

of being poked fun at. Most of the kids at school were really nice and Penelope actually enjoyed trying to communicate in different languages. Although, all classes were taught in English, some kids were from France, Sweden and all over the world and they did not speak English. 'Gosh, it is hard enough learning German,' she thought as she walked uphill. 'Someday I'll speak good enough German to tell that Marcus a thing or two.' Marcus was from Austria and seemed intent on making Penelope mad every day in class. She raised her fist in frustration, 'If he says one more thing about my size I am going to...' Suddenly, over her panting breath, she heard a tiny voice. Puzzled, she stopped her chewing and listened. It sounded like a faint voice was saying *"hilf mir."*[33]

Penelope yelled ahead to her sister, but Amelia had already rounded the corner. She peered about, eyeing the quiet group of tan houses all made of what looked like concrete but she saw no one. The voice had sounded like it was saying "help me." It also sounded very unhappy.

Shrugging her shoulders she started walking again, although she felt a little nervous and was relieved when she reached her driveway.

"Penelope Pond, what's taken you so long?" scolded her mother as she walked in the door. "Amelia said you were right behind her and that something must have happened to you. I have been so worried. And Tucker has been crying that he needs your help about something."

Penelope looked over at her sister and stuck out her tongue. "I was taking my time and I..." She was about to tell her sister

---

[33] Help me

about the secret voice but decided Amelia would continue her taunting so she stammered, "Uh, I have to…go help Tucker."

She ran up the spiral staircase to Tucker's room and found him sitting cross-legged on his bed, chin in hand. He looked so serious for a preschooler that she laughed out loud. "Tucker, what is it? Here I am. Do you need help with a puzzle or something?" she smiled. "Amelia is better at puzzles than me you know."

Tucker looked up at hearing Penelope's voice, jumped out of bed and hugged her tightly all in one motion.

"Peppy, the elf was looking for you. He climbed the tree but fell when he heard Mommy come upstairs. I think he was scared Mommy would yell at him." Tucker continued very fast. "I said you went to buy candy and you would be back in five hours 'cause you were ten and could run so fast and…"

"Five hours! You said I would be back in five hours! I wasn't even gone one hour, silly. Oh Tucker! Wait. Did you talk to this…this creature? He was here? Ohmagosh, what did he look like? Did you tell Mommy?" Penelope whipped around, yelling, "MOM! Tucker saw IT! Come here quick!"

Amelia and her mom both raced up the stairs to find Penelope in hysterics, shaking Tucker's shoulders.

"Calm down Penelope dear. Now, what is the matter? Is Tucker okay?"

"Mom, he saw IT. He TALKED TO IT." Penelope shouted and pointed at Tucker. "Ask him!"

Tucker started to cry and dove under the bed covers. "I want Daddy!" his muffled cry echoed under the bedspread. He started to thrash his legs about wildly.

"Penelope, see what you have done. He was fine today after school until you upset him. He is having a hard enough time adjusting to a new school. Why don't you go to your room and read a fairy tale? Write a story for school. Get it out of your system." Then, in a calmer tone, "Please honey. I realize everything is new for you too, but you are such a smart and clever girl and you are the…"

"Big sister. I know!" She wanted to cry or scream or do something but she could not move a muscle. She stared at the blank wall, ignoring her pleading mom, scowling sister, and sobbing brother. After five seconds, she ran to her room, leapt onto her bed, crying "Nobody loves me. Nobody believes me. Help me someone. Help me!"

She sat up with a start realizing she had said the very same words the voice had earlier. How strange. And then something stranger happened. 'Was she hearing an echo?' No, she cocked her head toward the window. She was hearing the same voice. Right now.

"Help me." It was faint but it was there. Slowly she raised her head from her tear-drenched pillow and looked out the window. It was coming from the pine tree.

Penelope craned her long thin neck forward, trying to see out her window without being noticed. She was scared to see who or what was out there. After all, how could everyone but her be so blind? At first glance she saw only the short pine needles sticking out of the stunted branches as usual. She let a small strand of matted hair fall from her mouth as she peered more closely. Nothing was moving on or near the tree, not even a cute, red German squirrel. The squirrels had the longest ears too, like rabbits. She was just about to turn away when she noticed the fingers. Only they were not like any fingers she had ever seen. They were chubby and short, but too chubby for little children and too short for adult fingers. They were covered in fuzzy yellow hair. And they were gripping her window ledge. She sucked in her breath until she couldn't breathe. She knew she should open the window but she was too stunned to move. She raised trembling hands to the glass and tapped it gently. The fingers didn't move. White knuckled, they held their grip. Moments sped by as Penelope stood paralyzed with shock.

"Amelia. Come here quick." she screamed but it came out as a frantic whisper. "HE'S HERE!" she finally managed to shriek.

Amelia came sauntering into their bedroom. "Mommy thinks you hate Germany. Do you want to go home?"

"AMELIA, OPEN THIS WINDOW NOW! HE'S THERE!" nodded Penelope, eyes flashing, at the window.

"Who's there, Penelope? The creature?" cried Amelia in disbelief as she ran over to the window and peered outside. "I don't see anything."

"Look down, silly. See his FINGERS!" she yelled between her teeth.

"I don't see anything, Penelope. Mommy is right. You're tricking us all." And with that, Amelia stormed out of the bedroom, thumping down the stairs.

Penelope frightened that the creature had disappeared or fallen by now and frightened also if he hadn't, looked down to see if the fingers were still there. "Ohmagosh" she gasped. "There's only a few left. He must be slipping." She quickly undid the hasp and opened the large window. Without hesitation, she grabbed the wrists and hoisted the attached body upwards.

"Oh my, this is so heavy," she thought as she pulled and pulled and hoped this fairy tale creature didn't bite.

Inch by hairy inch appeared as Penelope tugged on the strong, sinewy arms of the creature. Finally, through the long strands of her hair in her face, she saw its head. It managed to clamber over the window sill and hopped easily onto the bedroom carpet. They stood face to face. Well, almost. Penelope was taller and looked down...at him. It was a 'he.' That she was sure of. However 'what he was' was still a mystery. Where Penelope was slim and tall, the creature looked like he was a large, tall man who had somehow been shrunken and compressed into a compact, miniature version of a man standing three feet tall, or about a meter[34], she guessed. He did, indeed, have a beard and Penelope couldn't help but stare at its length and odd shape. 'Is he an elf or maybe he's really a dwarf with a beard like that?' she wondered. 'He could be a leprechaun I suppose.'

Brown and gray, it completely covered his face below his wide nose and reached the top of his bright green riding boots. But it didn't hang straight as one might expect. Rather it curved upward at the tip like a horn. Penelope followed the curve of the beard upward until she was looking into the crinkling eyes of the little man himself. She opened her mouth to speak but no sound came out. She saw that he was smiling, for huge white teeth made a glistening gap in his magnificent beard.

"Herzliche Grüsse an meine Freundin," [35]he stated and at once bowed low and swept the floor with his beard. With this statement he winked and held out his stubby but strong hand.

---

[34] A measurement in the metric system, a meter is 39.37 inches long.
[35] Hearty greetings to my friend

His deep voice moved up and down resonating like a cello. "I am called *Hochsternigen*[36] the Younger. I am descended from the Elvin Kings of Yore. I am the leader of all elves in Germany." He grasped her slender hand in his and stared into hers with bright black eyes. "On behalf of all my kinsmen and unborn descendents, I thank you. You saved me from trouble. I think not for the last time." And once more he bowed low, sweeping his beard across the floor. Then he said something quite odd. "You are the one we have been waiting for: the one to save all elves in Germany."

Penelope did not know what to do or say, but she felt no fear. She immediately thought 'He said he was an elf, didn't he?' She heard her lips mumble, "M...m...mmmee? Why... why me?" She frowned. "The one?" Feeling quite small and inadequate, she shrugged her shoulders, smiled and raised her eyebrows. She thought to herself she must be imagining this. It couldn't be real. Perhaps she was actually sleeping and dreaming. After all, she was only ten. She closed her eyes to be sure and reopened them in a blink only to discover that the 'elf' was indeed still there, and still smiling at her. She heard a low rumble and looked around until she realized that he was laughing. At her.

"My dear child of ten earthly years, I do not wish to alarm you. We are a gentle race. An Elfin prophecy told us you would come. Did you not see good elf, *Himmelwort* [37]the Large at the airport? I'm afraid it is becoming more and more difficult for him to conceal himself, even from other elves!" he chuckled. He scratched his beard in silence for a moment and then said,

---

[36] His name translates as High Stars
[37] His name translates as Heaven or Sky Word

"More will be explained at the forest meeting. I must go now and prepare the others. Once again, I welcome you, Penelope as you are called by humans. We have been waiting for you to appear in Germany. It is as the prophecy has foretold." With this he again bowed low, "Until we meet again on elfin soil. I must spread the news that you have arrived!!" Then he leapt onto the window sill and with a bound was climbing down the large pine tree. Penelope ran and looked down after him but by the time he had reached the ground he had disappeared. Vanished.

She sat down upon her bed in amazement. "Hoch... something," she remembered him saying. With a jolt she remembered he said she would learn more at another meeting, but he had forgotten to tell her where and when? "This is just too big." She got up and paced around the room. "I have got to tell Mommy and Daddy. MOM! DAD!" She screamed at the top of her lungs.

Both parents came bounding up the stairs urgently answering her call, "What is it Penelope? Are you hurt?" They gazed down at her with great concern in their eyes.

"HE WAS HERE AND HE IS AN ELF AND HIS NAME IS... Oh I forget...and he wants ME to help him and..." Penelope stopped suddenly noticing the look on each of their faces. "Okay, forget it. I will deal with this by myself. You will see. They only want ME to help them, anyway," she said in defiance.

In response, her mom and dad shook their heads, and headed back downstairs. She could hear the two of them mumbling words like 'elves, overtired, stressed-out, poor Penelope.'

25

Penelope sighed and leaned back on her elbows on her bed and contemplated what to do at the moment. She concentrated on remembering all Hoch-whoever had said to her. She, Penelope Pond, tall but meek girl of ten, was supposed to save the elves? So he was an elf. Save the elves in Germany? From what? And that great long beard? She laughed out loud thinking what her father would say, and then she shivered because it was real. This was really happening and she was alone. How would she prove to her family she was not a silly kid imagining crazy, fairytale stuff? She punched her pillow in frustration.

At that moment, Tucker popped his head into her room and said in a hurried whisper "Peppy, I heard the furry man talking to you, but I was scared to look..."

"Oh, Tucker. Are you the only one who believes me? Did you see him? He was here! A real-live elf! I must make everyone believe. This is too big for me..." she muttered as she paced back and forth across the room, pausing now and then to gaze out the window. At least she had one person who believed with her. It was a start, she supposed. Penelope felt like a cat that has finally swallowed the canary, but was unsure if it actually liked the taste. That night Penelope joined her family at dinner and acted like nothing was bothering her. She usually was a picky eater but she ate every bit of her *Schnitzel*.[38]

---

[38] Breaded pork cutlet

The Letter

Two weeks passed and still no sign or word from Hoch, as she now called the little man who called himself the leader of German elves. Penelope worried that Hoch had forgotten her, or decided that she was too young to help him. He was probably reading the wrong prophecy. She had looked up the strange word in the dictionary and it had said something about predicting the future. She sat at her desk at school and drew countless doodles and pictures of the elf, hardly bothering to listen to the German teacher's lesson on transportation vocabulary. She was so wrapped up in her thoughts that she didn't hear *Frau* Huybrechts[39] ask her a question until it was too late.

"I say it now for *zee tird* time, Penelope Pond, *vat* does *Hauptbahnhof* [40] mean in English?" Her strong German accent boomed across the classroom.

Before Penelope could collect her thoughts and answer with main train station, Marcus piped in with a sneer. "Yeah - Penelope thinks it means elves-are-in-this-room! She's probably talking to them in secret right now!" He slapped his desk and nodded with a smile to the other classmates.

---

[39] Ms. Huybrechts
[40] Main train station

To her horror, the whole class erupted into laughter and knowing giggles. She felt her eyes begin to water. This was worse than the taunts about her height. Now they think I'm crazy AND big! The tears started falling as Frau Huybrechts excused her from class to get herself together.

At home, Amelia, who normally would tease her for any strange behavior, tried to be nice to her. She even offered to buy her a candy after school at the post office.

"Okay, I'll walk down with you," she snapped at Amelia's pleading brown eyes. "Don't expect to see any elves," she added with hands on her hips. Somehow, Amelia's concern for her made her feel angry with herself.

Amelia merely skipped ahead eager for a treat. They entered the ever-busy small building and squeezed past those in line to scan the candy selection. Then, satisfied with their choices, they too joined the others in line to pay. They waited patiently behind a chatty lady who was picking up her dry cleaning. At last it was their turn and they spilled their goodies onto the counter and waited for Hexe's declaration of the price.

"*Zwei Euro Zwansig, bitte,*"[41] she clipped with tight lips. And then she did a very strange thing. When she gave the girls their change, she pressed a tiny envelope into Penelope's outstretched palm. "*Vorsicht!*"[42] She whispered and then in a louder voice for all to hear, she said *Danke. Auf Wiedersehen,*" and looked past the girls to the next customer.

Outside Amelia grabbed Penelope's arm. "What did 'the witch' say to you? She looked so mean all of a sudden. Did we have enough money?"

---

[41] Two Euros and twenty cents (€2, 20)
[42] Be careful

"Yes, of course. She wasn't mean, just, plain creepy. All she said was 'be careful'." Penelope debated whether to show her sister the secret envelope.

"I know she said something about me and you're not tellin'," ranted Amelia in a huff. "Just because you understand German. I...I hate Germany. It's not fair." And with that Amelia stomped away up the narrow cobble stoned road toward home.

Penelope, mouth open, watched her sister disappear round the corner. Realizing she was alone, she tore open the little letter, taking care not to rip it by mistake. Inside was a small white piece of paper with tiny, bright green handwriting. She squinted to make out the miniature script, written mostly in English.

A forest deep, a wood so bold
Finds us here. A tree so old
One field green, two so yellow,
Horses beware the stout little fellows.
Samstag um 13:00,
Hochsternigen the Younger

The last word, which was in German, made the most sense to Penelope, 'Saturday 13:00' or one p.m. The Germans used the 24 hour clock all the time. Instead of getting out of school at 3:00pm, they said at 1500. However, the other sentences before the time presented a confounding riddle. 'What does the note mean?' Penelope thought 'Why did Hexe slide it into my hand, and what does she know? The note sounded like directions to somewhere in the woods, but what old tree and which field?' There were so many of both around her village, Penelope didn't know where to begin. She jammed the note into the pocket of her jeans in frustration, and as she did she had a brilliant idea. She would show the note to her family as proof of the existence of Hoch and the elves.

The family's reaction was not what she expected, except for Amelia who claimed Penelope must have written it herself for attention. Penelope's hopes sank after dinner when she heard her parents talking in hushed tones in the living room.

"Janet, I think you are going too far with this. After all she's only a child. I did far worse stunts when I was a boy. I think this elf thing is kind of cute. In fact, everyone at work thinks so too. CargoLifter could use an imagination like hers," he added smiling.

"I thought it was cute as well, at first. But, honey, it has gone too far. It consumes all her thoughts and it is affecting her schoolwork. I realize she has had some trouble fitting in with some of the children, but now I'm concerned with her ability to recognize reality. They pick on her height and so on, and now the other school children tease her about her belief in elves! Mrs. Franchett even showed me some pictures Penelope had sketched at school. Elves, elves and more elves!" her mom said exasperated and threw up her hands.

"I don't see anything wrong with that. She's always loved to draw, and she is expressing her imagination and maybe she actually believes in them. That would be fine with me for now." Crouching low at the top of the stairs, Penelope raised her fist into the air in agreement with her dad.

"Ben, this is her math class assignment I'm talking about here. Not art class. I think we should look for outside help. We can't let Penelope go into an imaginary world when she needs to concentrate and learn important skills. She obviously needs some extra attention in helping her to adjust to this move to Europe. I spoke to the Head Mistress, Frau Walters, and she mentioned a wonderful counselor who has experience with such situations..."

Penelope's heart started pounding so loud she couldn't hear anything more. She sat back and tried to think. Just then, Amelia bounced from the bedroom the two girls shared.

"Penelope, can you help me with my homework? I don't know how to read a map."

Penelope cast a sideways glance at the primitive map her sister held. Not a real map, like the ones found in gas stations, this was comprised of large squares, each a different color. Some were light green, some a darker shade of green and some were bight yellow. In the center was a group of brown dots and next to the dots, a dark black circle. She was about to tell her sister to get lost when she noticed the map looked strangely familiar.

"Where did you get that? What do you have to do with this map?" She peered into Amelia's big brown eyes.

"Well, I found this in my cubby at school and my teacher said it probably is a farmer's map and I should try and figure out if it is a farm in our town. You know how good I am at puzzles," Amelia bragged. "She said I could write inside the squares what kinda crop was growing there and stuff. Daddy said the yellow squares look like what the Germans call '*Raps*'[43], you know, the fields we walked by when we went hiking last week, when I started sneezing like mad," she giggled and pointed at the map. "Maybe the green squares are the fields we pass on..."

"...ON THE WAY TO HORSEBACK RIDING!" shouted Penelope. "Amelia. You've done it! You've solved the riddle!" With this she stood up and gave Amelia a tight squeeze. "This map shows the way to the home of the elves. Look, I'll show you." She grabbed the map out of Amelia's hands and said in a rush. "Here are the two yellow fields and then another green one on the right. Straight ahead are the woods where we drive to horseback riding lessons. And this big black circle must be the meeting place! Now I know where to go on Saturday," she slapped the paper. Penelope was so excited she didn't notice the expression on Amelia's face.

"Penelope, this is MY map," and Amelia snatched the map back. "I got it at school. It is not your elf map." Then she became curious and thoughtful. "Can I come with you to look for the elves?"

"Only if you promise not to tell Mommy," Penelope confided to her sister, "She'll make me see a doctor or get a shot or something. We can ride our bikes so we won't be gone so long."

---

[43] Rape weed, a Eurasian plant cultivated for its seed used in oil

Saturday could not come soon enough for the two young explorers. After lunch they announced they were going on a bike ride. Amelia nearly gave their secret away several times, but was silenced each time with a scowl or nudge from Penelope. At the last moment however their plans were dashed when their dad spoke up.

"Great idea girls. Let's all take a bike ride."

With glum faces, the girls pedaled slowly behind their parents. Tucker waved at them with a big grin from his wagon towed behind his dad's bike. They slowly left the edges of the small town and headed toward the open green fields.

"Now what do we do, Penelope?" Amelia glanced over at her sister.

"I'll think of something." Penelope rode along trying to come up with a plan. When her mom asked in which direction they should ride, she knew she had the answer to her problem. First, she whispered to Amelia, "We gotta' get away from Mom and Dad, and quick. Get ready to fall off your bike. They will have to stop to help you and then we can speed away while they try to catch up. Penelope proceeded to yell aloud.

"Hey, I know a great path. Follow me everyone!" With the words, Penelope sped out in front of the family and pedaled furiously, widening the gap between them, so much that she could pretend not to hear their cries to slow down or to stop as they halted to help Amelia who had clumsily fallen off her bike.

If she could get to the meeting spot fast enough, Penelope could meet the elves in private. Surely Hoch didn't mean to invite the whole family?

A Circle in the Wood

Penelope was out of breath by the time she reached the horse stables where she and her sister rode. Now she had only to locate the 'black circle' on the map. She stopped and pulled out the crumpled note and looked around. She saw the riding hall and the stalls for the horses. Her gaze traveled down the dirt road a bit, to the small house in which her riding instructor, Herr Von Lehmden lived. She noted the funny-faced garden gnomes in front of the cottage as decoration.

She was about to continue her search when she remembered the riddle. "…horses beware the stout little fellows." Of course, that was it. She had thought the riddle was referring to the elves themselves. The schooling horses almost always became skittish when they passed these little plastic people who did, in fact, look a lot like elves. Now that she knew what elves looked like, of course. In a hurry, she hopped back on her bike and rode down the lane. Once past the garden she slowed and peered through the surrounding trees. "Humm," she thought aloud. "Somewhere is a big old tree." She looked skywards and turned around. "They all look big and old to me." Suddenly, through the columns of thick tree trunks, she saw a shaft of light where sunlight had managed to penetrate. Having no better idea where to look, she dismounted her bike and made her way through the trees toward the spray of light ahead. The pine needles crunched like dry cereal under her feet, breaking the still quiet in these woods. Although she was alone she had a strange feeling of being watched. With saucer-like eyes, she looked around and suddenly wished she had allowed her family to join her on this expedition.

Approaching the shaft of light, which seemed to always be a bit farther than she thought, Penelope noticed where the light met the ground forming a circle, there lay a group of rather large stones arranged precisely around the edge of light. It looked like a small room with a light shining overhead. Her eyes followed the tree trunks upwards in order to pinpoint the source of light. However, the sun proved too intense and she jerked her eyes away. Once again her gaze settled on the stone ring, but what a surprise! On each stone sat an elf. Startled, Penelope let out a small, muted, "Ohhh!"

"Freundliche Grüsse an unsere Penelope."[44] Penelope recognized the deep soothing voice of Hoch, greeting her in German. She stepped closer to the ring, shielding her eyes from the light with her hand, searching for his face. "We give you our most hearty welcome." With this, Hoch hopped off his rock seat and bowed low with his broad sweeping gesture. Although this time, Penelope was able to see the bow performed several times as each elf jumped off his rock, one by one, and swept the forest floor with his beard. This took awhile as she counted four elves and, at the same time, she noticed there were five stones. As if he could read her mind, Hoch nodded at her and

---

[44] Friendly greetings to our Penelope.

then the empty stone. Penelope took his cue, and sat down upon the fifth stone.

Penelope felt all elfin eyes upon her. Unsure what to do or say, she stammered a small, "Hello."

At once, each elf began speaking to her. She was not able to understand anything because each one tried to outdo the other. She was too polite to say 'stop,' although she wanted to cover her ears.

Not needing to read her mind, Hoch silenced the noise with a raised hand. He smiled and spoke to her, "Please forgive my countrymen in their excitement to meet you. They have long awaited this day, and when you greeted them in their tongue of birth, they were unable to restrain their mirth."

Penelope was confused and it must have showed on her face. Hoch continued, "Listen with your heart, my child, and you will understand all we say. You are hearing and speaking in Elf speak, the magical language of elves. These sacred stones allow those who sit upon them to enter our world and speak and hear as one of us. Let us begin with Himmelwort the Large. I believe you two may have already met," he added with a wink.

Penelope's attention was drawn across the circle to a stone on which a large elf, indeed, sat. In his case, "Large" referred to his waist size. In fact, when he stood to speak, she saw he was as wide as he was tall. More noticeable than his girth was his clothing. He looked very fancy, like her Dad when her parents went to a dance party. He wore a shiny, black suit with a ruffled, white shirt. However, the bright green bow tie and matching, glow-in-the-dark-green shoes was what really made him stand out. Suddenly, she recalled an image at the airport of a chubby elf in a pink ballet outfit. Could it be? She was too embarrassed to ask.

"I greet you, most special one. Unlike my fellow country-elves here," he cast a scornful look around the circle, "I wished to greet you in a style and manner befitting your honored position. At least I will not let good taste and classic fashion-sense die out before our race does…die out, that is." He cleared his throat and finished with another sweeping bow. Only this time, a loud tearing sound shattered the quiet forest.

Himmelwort stood up fast with round eyes and mouth in an 'O' shape. The other elves began laughing and pointing at the fat elf's backside. Penelope put her hand over her mouth and tried not to laugh. Quite embarrassed, Himmelwort scooted back to his rock and sat down.

"He's always ripping his clothes," announced a third elf, now standing to her left. "If he would stop picking all the *Himbeeren*[45] and making pies to eat, he wouldn't get so fat!"

This new elf, Penelope noticed, was in better shape, at least for an elf. He wore green boots like Hoch's and the simple brown jacket and pants. She wanted to make a good impression so she nodded, smiling, in his direction. Her polite gesture was not well received.

"There is nothing to smile about here. Oh, no sirreee. We are doomed you see, and if you can't help us…I…I don't know what we will do. Help. Help us. You must…Oh no…" He continued to rant and sob until Hoch again used his hand to silence him. It worked like a switch.

---

[45] Raspberries

"You must excuse elf *Mondwagen*[46]. He is our professor and is learned in the ancient secrets and knowledge of the elf kingdom. He wants what's best for us, but he tends to get carried away and worries about everything." Hoch then nodded to the elf on Penelope's right. "On the other hand, *Liedersinger*[47] here, is a more cheerful...umm?" Hoch paused for a brief second, "...fellow, and usually has a song to brighten the darkest forest."

Liedersinger, a rather skinny elf she thought, and unlike the others, did not have a beard. He started to sing in a high, clear voice, but was silenced as well by the hand of Hoch. "Later, my friend, there will be time for song. I must share our story and explain our problem to Penelope." He cleared his throat and spoke out to the forest with arms open.

"For years beyond the range of man, elves have inhabited the earth. Our colonies are scattered across the lands and thousands of elves have made up our Kingdom. There are many kinds of elves. We are Wood Elves, and as you might guess, reside in deciduous forests all over Earth. Some say we resemble dwarves because of our beards and great strength. In truth, we Wood Elves were a separate civilization which intermarried with the Dwarf species. As the Dwarf population became extinct, our two civilizations evolved into one. A clever few refer to us as "Dwelves," he chuckled. "We are a hardy folk and have survived for many millennia. We have learned to live side by side with humans, minding their curious ways always staying out of their way.

---

[46] Moon Wagon or Car
[47] Song Singer

You see, long ago humans believed in elves. Although we never completely lived as a community or shared a dinner table together, humans and elves have existed as friendly, but distant, neighbors. In fact, one helped the other in times of need. For example, we learned about forging metals, iron and bronze, from your human people. In turn, we shared our knowledge of herbs and plant life. The healing power of elves is renowned. Humans may not have realized what and how much information we have given them, but..." Hoch's speech was interrupted by Mondwagen's screech,

"And now look what the ungrateful humans are doing. They're trying to KILL us!"

Again, Hoch's hand went up. "Human child, let me explain. We have lived in harmony for thousands of years, until the rapid advances humans made in industry and technology superseded and overtook the need for harmony with the elves. People no longer believe in our very existence, and if a human does not believe in our existence, they cannot see or speak with us. Because of this disbelief, they don't know we are living amongst them, and they are destroying our homes. Blind to the terrible harm they cause, they nevertheless, are destroying our civilization." Hoch paused and bowed his head. A low moan from Liedersinger broke the silence.

Penelope noticed that Liedersinger had balled his slender hands into fists. She turned her head back to listen to Hoch.

"As we sit here, deep in the wood, in a circle hidden, our elf wives and daughters remain underground. They must hide from the iron hand of humans. Too many elf babies and young have died as man has cleared the forests, smashing and maiming their little bodies, in the name of progress." Hoch cried and stared into Penelope's wide eyes.

Penelope sat still, concentrating on every word. "But, I don't understand," she asked, "How are humans hurting you?"

"Forests across this great earth are cut down for wood, fuel, houses, roads and space for humans," he answered. "Have you learned yet about the devastation to the Rain Forests? Our brethren elves there had to flee years ago, because they could not outrun the bulldozers and the burning acres of jungle." He pointed to Liedersinger, "We believe Liedersinger to be the single surviving Rain Forest Elf."

Liedersinger on cue, bowed and nodded solemnly, but Penelope could see fire in his light blue eyes. 'That explains why he looks different from the others,' she decided to herself.

Hoch continued, "On the vast plains of the northern continents, corn and wheat crops have replaced entire elfin communities, now lost forever. Alpine Elves, white and as light as snow have receded as have the mighty glaciers into history. Elves, from across the planet have migrated here to the deep woods of Germany for our last stand. Many humans are concerned about animal extinction, but they do not realize they have nearly exterminated the elf race." Hoch was red in the face. He paused for effect and then uttered:

"We elves, here in Germany, are all that is left of elfin civilization."

"Why don't you try and talk to the people in charge and tell them to stop because they are hurting you and all the elves?"

"*Ach, meine kleine Maus!*"[48] Mondwagen wailed. "That is impossible. Humans do not believe in us. Therefore they cannot see or hear us!"

"I am surprised they cannot hear your ranting, friend Mondwagen," Hoch winked at Penelope. "However, he speaks the truth. Humans have crossed so far over into the realm of machines, the world of supercomputers and have stressed our living environments and communities by overdevelopment of the Earth's natural resources. They are unable to imagine a reality that includes elves. They believe they have all the answers to the Natural World: too much carbon dioxide and the effect on Global Warming and so on. They are as oblivious to the great damage they are inflicting upon this earth and to themselves as they are to the existence of elves. If they can't find what they seek on a computer," he spat out the word computer like it was the plague, "it must not exist." He waved his hand as if to brush away the other elves in the circle.

"How do you know they ever saw you?" Penelope couldn't resist asking.

"That is a good question. We do know people believed in us by the number of stories and tales written about elves. Though considered "Fairy Tales" by human critics today, those stories were astonishingly accurate in their depiction of us."

Unable to control himself, Himmelwort blurted, "And don't forget those awful little, plastic creatures, humans put in their gardens. Why on earth would they want ridiculously dressed, fabricated dummies with bad taste, dotting their doorways? Imagine," he sighed, mouth open, "wearing overalls? How

---

[48] Oh my little mouse!

gauche![49] What a fashion *faux pas!*[50] I wouldn't be caught dead..."

She realized then he was talking about the garden gnomes seen everywhere in the area. She suppressed a giggle. He would have continued rambling like this had not Hoch used his silencing hand.

Penelope, feeling a bit overwhelmed, asked with a slight tremor in her voice, "What do you want *me* to do?"

Hoch cast a quick glance at his countrymen and then turned to Penelope with such a serious expression the entire forest seemed heavy with silence and expectation.

Just then, a sound like metal scraping pavement shattered the moment. She glanced through the trees to her far left and spied Amelia, untangling herself from her bike. Amelia looked up and, despite the distance, the sisters' eyes met.

"Penelope! What are you doing in there?" She crunched toward the circle. Then, in a loud whisper, "Did you find the elves? Mommy and Daddy said for me to come find you and bring you home. They're kinda mad."

Penelope could tell her sister was grinning with the last statement. She wanted to answer but she held her tongue. Let Amelia see for herself.

Amelia came crashing through the woods, dodging tree trunks in her way like a slalom skier. Penelope could see the anticipation on her sister's face and felt excited for her. She would welcome a fellow believer.

"Penelope, why did you leave me...behind? I got right up and you were gone."

---

[49] Vulgar
[50] Mistake

"I'm sorry, Amelia. I had to get away. Besides, I knew you'd catch up. I had to speed off faster. They would never believe this..." Penelope made a sweeping gesture with her arm indicating the stone-rimmed circle. "These are...my... elf friends. This is...is Hoch and he is..."

"Penelope. What are you talking about? What elf friends? All I see is a bunch of dumb rocks in the sun."

Penelope was stunned. She looked around the circle, noting each elf on his rock, and when she came to Hoch, she asked with a puzzled expression, "Hoch, you are here, aren't you? Why can't she see you?"

"Remember child, only believers can see and hear us."

"Yes, but Amelia really wants to see you. She definitely believes in you."

"There is a difference between 'wanting to' and actually believing in someone or something," he answered, rubbing his beard-covered chin. "This is the source of our current problem, you see. If humans would allow themselves to imagine and broaden their narrow perception of life on earth, they would be able to believe in us, and thus, see us. Right now, all they can think of is progress, wealth and industry. We have tried to make humans believe, but we find their hearts are not open." Hoch's face looked sad, but then it brightened, "That is why we need you, dear child, untainted and innocent, to convince your people, elves are real. You see, an Elfin Prophecy..."

Penelope had been listening so closely, she forgot about her sister. When she looked over at her sister, Amelia was standing, arms crossed in front of her chest, with her head tilted at an odd angle. Her eyes were dark slits.

"Penelope, who are you talking to? I don't see anyone. There is nothing there!" she cried pointing. I'm going home," and she turned to leave.

"Wait, Amelia! I am not kidding you. The elves are here and they are in trouble. No one can see them, and they need people to see them. And, it's a long story. Please don't go," Penelope begged. She spun around to the elves, eyes pleading, "Hoch, Himmelwort. Please help me. How can I make her see?"

"Tell her to sit down, legs crossed, eyes closed," answered Mondwagen in an unusually calm and wise voice, quite different from the wailing Penelope witnessed earlier. "She must listen to the forest, feel the ancient earth beneath her, and smell the wood. Let the damp air cool her face and carry her mind into our world. If her heart is open, Amelia will open her eyes and see just as you do."

Penelope said to Amelia. "Wait, Amelia! Please try something for me. You will see I am not dreaming, and you will also be able to see and hear the elves! Please trust me!" She had a hard time convincing Amelia to try this, but was finally able to coax her by also agreeing to participate herself. The two girls sat still, under the great trees, feeling the forest around them. In a soft voice, Liedersinger began to sing a mournful sounding tune. Penelope looked closely at Liedersinger as if something was not quite right but was soon overwhelmed by a feeling that she was somewhere very old, back in time, back before people roamed the earth. She felt the seasons, and the vast power of nature. She felt the earth shudder, and she shivered. She felt a trembling hand grasp hers.

"Penelope," whispered Amelia, "where are we? I feel cold and warm at the same time. Hey, who is THAT...?" she exclaimed in amazement.

Just then, a huge crash ripped through the dead quiet. The girls jumped up and screamed. A huge earthmover was taking down trees a stone's throw away and the trees were cracking, splitting and falling like giant dominoes. Leaves and dirt clouded the air, making seeing difficult. Penelope grabbed her sister and watched, in horror, as a huge, old pine started leaning in their direction. She shrieked at the elves, "Watch out!" just in time for them to dash to safety.

Hoch grabbed her by both arms and screamed, "RUN. You are in great peril. We cannot risk losing you, child. Now you see, by your own eyes, the destruction around us. You see your task before you; you must do all you can to stop the construction of the new high-speed rail line, the ICE train. Even its name brings shivers to our hearts. The tracks will cut directly through our homes here in the wood. We have nowhere else to go. Our civilization's magic is based here. We are unable to leave this spot on earth, and we cannot let it be destroyed, or we will not be able to live or breathe. Please child! Convince the humans we exist and to move the line elsewhere. It is our only chance of survival. Your task is great, but I see you can. You have already caused one human to believe in our plight," he panted, nodding towards Amelia. "The prophecy holds true! It is you who can save us, and our ancestors have brought you to us at this time of great need. I must go now and see to the safety of our elfin families in the woods nearby. I need to let them know we have a chance to be rescued from extinction!"

Penelope stood there as still as a frightened deer. She wondered briefly why Hoch said she had already caused one human to believe in their plight. 'He must mean Tucker,' she thought. She then noticed Amelia was standing, silent, with both hands covering her mouth and had her eyes wide open in a fixed stare. She looked like she was about to scream. With the terrible scene of earthmovers before them in the forest, and the falling trees, Amelia had good reason to be terrified reckoned Penelope. She pulled quickly at Amelia's arm to get her to run for their bikes. She then turned to wave goodbye to Hoch and the other four elves, but they were already gone.

Pedaling fast at first, and then in slow motion toward home, the girls had time to reflect. Penelope felt shaky and unsteady on her bike. She felt horrible that she put Amelia in harm's way, and wondered what her sister was thinking. Worse, what would she tell their mother and father about the forest and her continued belief in elves? "Gosh, Amelia, we were almost killed. I'm sorry I dragged you into this. You must think I am really nuts, now. I am so sorry. "

Amelia remained quiet. Penelope was quiet also, and concerned. Then, after a couple of minutes, Amelia stuttered, "Was…was one of the elves wearing a penguin costume?"

Penelope skidded to a stop. "Ohmagosh, Amelia, you really did SEE THE ELVES? See what I mean, they ARE real. And they need our help. Hoch is like the leader and now you know him, too. Mondwagen, or something, I think it means 'moon wagon', is so strange. And Himmelwort is called 'the Large' and boy is he ever…" Penelope calmed down a bit and scratched her head looking into Amelia's big brown eyes, "Amelia, did you really see something?"

46

The most wonderful words Penelope heard since moving to Germany reached her ears, "Penelope, I believe you now. I always wanted to believe you, but I never saw them until now. ELVES! This is so awesome…" Amelia spread her arms wide.

Penelope interrupted her, "The Express Train. I don't know how I can do it. How can I stop a train? I mean stop the construction through the elf forest?" She looked at Amelia with questioning eyes as the reality of the problem sank in deeper. "I'm a kid…" she sighed.

"Penelope, I can help you. Remember, I figured out the map. I can't wait to tell Mommy and Daddy and my friends about the elves." With mounting excitement, Amelia rode off across the fields toward home.

Penelope remained behind and watched her sister and her bike get smaller and smaller. She shook her head and said aloud, "She's gonna learn the hard way. No one's gonna believe her, she'll see. Plus she'll probably get me into even more trouble with Mom and Dad." Feeling tired and very small, Penelope pedaled up the hill with what felt like the weight of the world on her slender shoulders. She wondered what in the world the 'Prophecy' said about the future… and her part to play?

A Warning

Penelope slowed her horse named Sonny to a walk around the enclosed ring with the other students in her riding lesson. Nothing betrayed the terrible turmoil she felt inside. Were the elves okay? Why didn't Hoch make contact? Did the elfin families get hurt? And, most of all how was she, Penelope Pond, going to stop the German construction crews from doing their job of building a high-speed rail-line through the forest? Suddenly the harsh voice of Herr Von Lehmden reached her ears.

"Arbeits-Temperatur Bitte! Pass Auf Amerikanerin! Schläfst du?"[51] He screamed waving his hands. Startled, Penelope immediately brought Sonny to a trot and paid attention. She was afraid of Herr Von Lehmden and his anger, but she realized he only wanted the best from his students. And he yelled at all of them equally. The German students were just as fearful of him as she. Penelope trotted obediently around the ring trying hard to maintain a trot and avoid Herr Von Lehmden's wrath. She would worry about the elves later.

On Thursday during German class, she received a small glimmer of hope in her search to help the elves. Her teacher,

---

[51] Working trot please! Pay attention American girl! Are you sleeping?

Frau Huybrechts announced that the German class would study, along with Mrs. Merkel's social studies class, the subject of transportation. She explained how language and communication were an important part of transportation. However, Penelope's hope soared when her teacher added that they were taking a special field trip to visit the construction site of the new Intercity Express or ICE Train tracks. She learned that the new rail line was to connect the cities Frankfurt and Cologne. 'Wow, this is my chance to see the actual place the elves are talking about. Maybe there will be something at the construction site to give me an idea as to how to help them?'

Penelope could not focus on anything else the rest of the week. The trip was scheduled for the next Tuesday, and she twisted her hair into fine knots in anticipation. Cross-legged on her bed, she and her new confidante, Amelia, made plans and speculated as to what Penelope might do. The relationship between the two sisters was now a lot closer now that they both shared the secret of the elves.

"Penelope, this is for grown-ups. We're just kids. We can't make them stop their diggers," was all Amelia could offer.

"If this is for grown-ups, how come Mommy and Daddy didn't believe you when you told them 'bout the elves, huh?" chided Penelope. "Grown-ups think this is all make-believe. That is why it is up to us!"

"I can't believe my best friend Jessie won't believe me either. She even believes in the tooth fairy," muttered Amelia.

"You see, it is only you and me. Well...Tucker says he believes too, but he is too small to help. Humm, we need a plan, but first," Penelope uncrossed her legs and hopped off the bed, "I need some candy to think. Let's go to the post office."

The girls walked down the hill to buy goodies. For once, the small shop was empty of customers. The post lady looked up from her papers and eyed the girls.

Penelope and Amelia felt her strong gaze upon their backs as they pondered over the candy selection. When they turned around to pay, they were surprised when she whispered in a hurried rush, "You must beware of my son. *Er ist ein herzensguter Mann.*[52] You can help *Klaus-Dieter. Bitte!* [53] You must help him before he does great harm." She was about to continue, but an old man entered the post office and she stopped talking.

Penelope and Amelia looked at each other with raised eyebrows. The post lady took their money and bade them a rushed *Auf Wiedersehen* and signaled with her hands for them to leave.

Outside, both girls spoke at once. "What did she say? Who is her son?" They opened their candies and walked up the steep street.

"Maybe he's a killer on the loose," sputtered Amelia. "She said he did great harm."

"Actually she said we must stop him before he does great harm. Great harm? To us? She said something about his heart when she said *herzi-something,*" reflected Penelope, sucking on a gummi bear. "I wonder why we should beware of him. Is he evil? Where is he anyway?" She looked around as if she might see him hiding behind a hedge.

"She said he was a good man too. That's what *'hair-tsee-guter'* means. I know. I learned that in German," bragged Amelia. Then, as an afterthought, "Maybe he knows something…"

---

[52] He is a nice man.
[53] Klaus-Dieter is a German first name. Please!

"ABOUT THE ELVES!" finished Penelope almost choking. "She was the one who gave us the note in the first place! She must know something, too!" Turning to Amelia, "Do you think Hoch is her son? He seems so nice and true and…." Penelope's thoughts drifted off.

"No way, Penelope. She said his name, something that sounded like Mouse Peter. Hoch is an elf and the post lady is definitely a human. They can't be related."

"You're right, Amelia. But she does know something. Something important."

Elves Live Here!

By Sunday night, both Penelope and Amelia were becoming frustrated in their efforts to come up with a workable plan for Penelope's class trip to the ICE train site. Even after many trips to the post office, they were still not able to find out any more from the post lady. Either someone else was working or there were too many other customers there at the same time. Strangely, during each visit she had seemed more and more nervous with their presence.

"Okay, Amelia. This is it. We have no more time. What can I do on the class trip? Jump up and down; scream Elves live here?" With this, Penelope began jumping on her bed, chanting the words over and over.

Amelia, too, joined in the fun, jumping and thrashing about on her bed. "Elves live here, elves live here, el…"

She choked on her last word when she saw her mom's darkened face in the doorway. "Oh! Hi Mom, Penel' and I were just talkin' 'bout the elves and…"

"Lights out. Get right to bed, girls. I have heard so much about elves I can't stand it anymore. Penelope, I made an appointment Tuesday for you and me to meet with the school counselor. We are going to get to the bottom of this elf…thing." With that, Mrs. Pond turned and headed back downstairs.

Stunned, the girls stared wide-eyed at one another. Then in unison came, "Tuesday, no, not Tuesday!"

"Penelope, what are you going to do? You *must* go to the construction site." Amelia crossed her arms in front of her chest. "I'm tellin' Mom she needs to listen to us. I'm going to demand it."

"Wait, Amelia. That will make it even worse." She looked around the room. "I wish Hoch were here to tell me what to do."

Downstairs, they heard their parents murmuring. Suddenly, the shrill double beep of the phone interrupted them. The girls listened to their mother answer, and then try to speak German with the caller. "*Was ist es? Ein Problem? Wo?*"[54] They heard her say. She hung up with the words, "*Okay, bis Dienstag, hier, um neun Uhr.*"[55]

They heard their mom's footsteps on the stairs. She entered their room, shaking her head. "That was the strangest thing. Some man named *Herr Hoch* called and said he was a *Schornsteinfeger* [56]and had to clean the chimney. He must do it this Tuesday. Apparently, it's some kind of law here that you must have your chimney cleaned every year. One more rule doesn't surprise me but I guess we'll have to change your appointment at school, Penelope. He did say the strangest thing too. He said that he would be as quick as a team of elves. What a funny thing to say? If he only knew." Mrs. Pond laughed,

---

[54] What is it? A problem? Where?
[55] Okay, until Tuesday, here at nine o'clock.
[56] Chimney Sweep

shrugged and hugged her daughters. "You two look like you've seen a ghost. Time for bed. *Gute Nacht. Ich habe euch lieb.*"[57]

The sisters turned to one another. Penelope whispered, "How did Hoch know? He must have been listening." She glanced at the tree outside the window. "Guess we'll find out something on Tuesday." The girls smiled to each other across the large bedroom and giggled as they climbed into their beds.

---

[57] Good night. I love you.

The Construction Site

"Now remember *Kinder*[58], do not touch anything in the work area. These men have an important but dangerous job putting in this high speed rail line. We are to stay out of their way and observe." The teacher continued her lecture, pointing out German words used in travel while the students ignored her, whispering to one another and bouncing happily on the plush seats of the school bus.

Twisting her hair, Penelope looked out the window. Was Hoch going to be there?

"Was suchst du, Penelope?[59] Her seatmate, Katja, leaned over and interrupted Penelope's thoughts.

"Oh, nothing really, Katja. Just trees and stuff," she pointed. She could sense that Katja was not ready to hear the word elves in any language. She was about to give up her search when she spied movement in the trees. Looking closer, she saw a small line of short people walking through the pine trees. She wiped her eyes. The elves! They were marching toward the construction zone. Each one appeared to be carrying something in his hand. Silently, Penelope gave the thumbs up sign.

---

[58] children
[59] What are you looking for, Penelope?

The bus slowed and turned onto a dirt road. They passed signs with big red slashes saying *"Verboten"*[60] and *"Baustelle"*[61]. The volume on the bus grew to a crushing roar. Frau Huybrechts held up her hand as the bus lurched to a stop. Her voice boomed out, "QUIET EVERYONE." But at the same time, everyone had already become quiet with curiosity, so that hers was the only loud voice echoing throughout the bus. Her voice sounded so loud and angry like a screeching owl that all other sounds became mute. The children snickered as the construction workers looked up in shock. Then, with a visibly red face Frau Huybrechts whispered, "Remember, do not disturb the workmen."

Penelope bounded off the bus and craned her neck to see the construction and discover how it was causing the destruction of the elfin population.

As far as she could see, a huge swath of trees had been cleared, creating a tornado–like effect upon the landscape. Giant yellow earthmovers, diggers and cranes crawled about like bugs, gnawing and kneading the bare brown earth. Dwarfed by the machinery, men in bright orange overalls scurried about pulling cables, directing long steel beams, and yelling at one another. Clouds of blue smoke from cigarettes rose here and there. It looked like a war zone.

Penelope shook with a sudden chill. How could she stop all this! Her wide eyes scanned the destruction's edge, seeking refuge in the dark woods. Hoch, Liedersinger, Mondwagen, where are you?

---

[60] Forbidden
[61] Construction zone

"Ach du liebe Güte! Was ist hier denn los!"[62] Penelope heard the angry words from the crane driver nearby. She looked over and saw her class and teacher forming a circle around something. They were all shaking their heads. Some kids were laughing.

A tall, blond haired man was addressing them. First he pointed at something on the ground and then upwards at the crane. She ran over to find out. The man was explaining,

"As chief engineer on this very important project, it is my duty to insure safety on the site. You can see that this was a harmless mistake. Although my men will not be happy about losing their lunches, they will be thankful it was only their *Schnitzel* and *Bratwürste*[63] squashed and not their heads!"

Penelope peered into the mess before her. Sure enough, it was a pile of lunch boxes with the contents flattened and splattered everywhere. The crane had dropped a hunk of concrete right on top of them. She too felt a giggle bubbling up inside of her. Just before it popped out, she noticed a glimmer of light from the trees.

It was the glint from Himmelwort's trendy sunglasses. Even from her distance, she could see he was outfitted for a safari, wearing a tight fitting tan shirt and matching shorts. Roped around his stout neck were binoculars and he even sported a pith helmet, a hard kind of helmet that lion hunters wore in old jungle movies. She had to smile. He looked ridiculous, but she was glad to see him nonetheless. He was waving her over to him. She looked over her shoulder and made a dash to the shadow of the wood.

---

[62] Oh for the love, what's going on here?
[63] sausages

"Himmelwort, I'm so glad you're okay." She tried to give him a hug but her arms went only half the way around. "Are Hoch and the others here as well? I just don't know what to do out here. I mean, these are real machines and all. How can I stop them? And that chief man, the one over there," she pointed, "he looks so mean and serious and..."

"Penelope, darling. Don't worry. Hoch has a plan. What a plan! You are going to convince Mr.-Chief-Engineer," Himmelwort said his name like a kid would say 'sissy-face', "that he cannot build a train line here 'cause these woods and earth are cursed." Himmelwort ended with a wink.

"A curse? That's not true. How can we say such a thing? No one will believe me," she answered, gesturing toward the earthmovers.

"Well, I for one would feel cursed if someone or something crushed my lunch. Hit an elf where it hurts," he added, rubbing his belly. "Hate to see anything disrupt this pretty picture of progress here," he said, pointing in little circles at the site.

"Himmelwort, you mean the elves caused the crane to drop the block on the lunches? Wow, that's neat. But, you don't mean you and the elves are going to...to sabotage the construction area?" Her fingers twisted her hair into ringlets. "Someone could get hurt. I can't let you do that."

"Penelope, calm down. No self-respecting elf would ever purposely hurt anything, even a diabolical human like *Herr Briefträger*."[64] Himmelwort pointed toward the Chief Engineer. "That guy needs to lighten up. He could also use a few fashion

---

[64] Mr. Letter Carrier

tips. That orange jumpsuit is so *passé.*"[65] Himmelwort pursed his lips and shook his head.

Just then, he and Penelope were jolted back to the scene at hand by a large bang followed by a thud like an earthquake and finished off with a strange hissing sound.

"Was ist los?"[66] They heard Herr Briefträger scream. A large earthmover had plowed into a parked dump truck, and knocked it over, dirt, stones and mud. But that was not all. The sludge poured out and onto the workmen's parked cars. Some were completely covered, oozing black gook from their windows.

Penelope looked at Himmelwort with new respect. "Did the elves do that too?" She looked around hoping to see one of the merry fellows in action. What she did see was Herr Briefträger losing his cool. He was yelling, pointing and practically pirouetting around the overturned truck. She also spied her Frau Huybrechts huddling with the class near the bus. She appeared to be worried. Penelope realized that she must be looking for her. She decided to remain 'lost' for awhile longer. She knew she had a job to do.

"Where are Hoch and the rest?" she asked Himmelwort.

Well, Mondwagen was helping that worker drive the front loader-backhoe," Himmelwort answered winking one eye. "Only the driver didn't know it. Too bad the fellow misplaced his glasses." Himmelwort slapped himself heartily on the knee. "Liedersinger is adjusting the radio frequencies on their walkie-talkies. She always changes the stations, looking for an elfin tune she can dance to." He added, winking, "It's a shame

---

[65] So out of fashion
[66] What's going on?

it interferes with their important communications so they are unable to talk to one another."

Penelope just stared at Himmelwort. It was obvious he didn't realize what he had just said. Liedersinger, Liedersinger was a girl. A FEMALE ELF. She started to blurt out her discovery, but caught the stern gaze of Hoch telling her to remain silent. Instead she stuttered the words, "I uh, I understand Hoch's plan now." Penelope stood with her hand on her chin. "If things start to go wrong for no reason, we can tell him it is the work of elves. There will be no other way to explain it. He has got to believe."

"Plus, dear child, he won't be able to finish his 'really important project'," Himmelwort pushed out his already large mid-section and began to swing his hips, "because we elves are so..."

"So committed to the safety and security of our people," interrupted Hoch with a small cough. "Penelope, I see Himmelwort has apprised you of our plan. He nodded gently. And, I see that the time is here for you to do your part." Hoch pointed to Herr Briefträger, whose sleek, orange overalls were now covered in mud from trying to dig out his car from under the dumped sludge.

The construction chief stood shaking his head and slowly raised his walkie-talkie radio to his lips. Penelope could tell he was giving instructions to another worker, but she couldn't hear his words. His whole expression changed though, from frustration to shocked disbelief. She and her elfin fellows followed his gaze.

Off in the distance, at the entrance to a newly built tunnel, tiny explosions were taking place. Bit by bit, large chunks of reinforced concrete block were dropping off the tunnel walls, creating an avalanche effect.

"Mein Gott, was soll das?" [67] Cried Herr Briefträger, head in hands.

"Penelope. Go to him. It is now time to tell him about us", coaxed Hoch. "His ears are open." Then, he added with a wink, "Oh, and mention my name."

Penelope walked across the packed earth, skirting cables and construction equipment. Seeking reassurance, she turned and looked back now and then, at her elfin friends. They waved her on. Himmelwort looked like he was praying. For courage, she grabbed a thick wad of hair and twisted it with both hands. When she was within five feet of the chief, she stopped and in her old habit, slouched her back and seemed to shrink. "Ah – umm" was all she could manage when he failed to notice her. *"Entschuldigen Sie,"*[68] Then, in English, "Excuse me, sir?" Her feet scuffed the ground. "Hello, my name is Penel…"

"Was? Oh. Hau ab, Kleine!"[69] He raised his hand and turned.

"Wait. *Bitte,* Herr Briefträger. I am here to help. I know why things are going wrong. I…"

He whipped around and said between his teeth, "You *know* something. If you children have played games with my site, I WILL HAVE YOU…!" he raised his hands into fists.

"No, no. That's not it. It is not children, but the work of elves. Elves are small and they live…"

"Elves?" Then, with piercing, squinty eyes, "What do you know of elves?"

---

[67] My god, what is that?
[68] Excuse me
[69] Oh it is only you, little one. Go away

"I know they live, here. And that you are destroying their homes with this rail line. Hoch and his people only want to live in peace. You must…"

"Elves! Such talk is nonsense. Do you think I am a child, you silly girl?" He threw down his radio and started walking away.

"WAIT! Surely you know the name *Hoch…sternigen?*" Penelope said with a slight sneer. This man was making her mad and she was determined to help the elves. Amazing, but she no longer felt afraid. She stood up straight and tall, making use and now proud of her too tall height.

She saw him pause in his step. She rushed on, "Yes, that's right. Hochsternigen, the leader of the elves. He sent me to talk to you." She paused, and then gambled on a hunch. "He remembers you too!"

Herr Briefträger halted in his tracks. Penelope could see that he recognized the name and it affected him greatly. His face was bright red in harsh contrast to his yellow hair and black eyes that sunk into his skull like two holes. He began turning his head as if looking for a ghost.

She decided to play her ace. "Look! Over there by the trees. Hochsternigen and the elves have come to see you." She pointed at the elves, which were now looking quite serious, lined in rows, hands on hips, at the edge of the wood.

At first, she wasn't sure if Herr Briefträger did, indeed, see the elves. She was taking a chance that he believed enough to be able to see the elves. Herr Briefträger took one look at the freakish sight and screamed.

"IT IS A CURSE! It can't be so. They were only a childhood fantasy, a dream. *Ach du liebe Güte!* [70] I have gone mad."

He started sobbing. Poor Penelope felt awkward trying to soothe this hardened, older man, but she felt she had to say something kind.

"Sir, I know this is weird, but it is true." She patted his muscled, hairy arm. "At first, I didn't believe my own eyes either. The elves came to me and I was the only one who could see them. My family still doesn't believe me. Well, except my sister, Amelia, and my little brother, but he's only four. The elves are gentle and kind and mean you no harm. They only wish to live in harmony with us. Hoch asked me to help them and sent me to explain the problem to you. You can help."

"What problem?" Herr Briefträger looked up. "If it's about the elf fantasies of my youth, I cannot help you." His speech became odd and high pitched and made Penelope nervous. "*Mutter* [71]always told me the elves would come back. I thought she was joking with me. When I was a boy, I used to tell my mother tales of elves. At first, she thought I was crazy." He looked up at the sky. "Who's crazy now?" He looked down at Penelope. "So, you are the new chosen one." He emphasized chosen.

"Well, I don't know. All I know is you have got to stop construction here. You are destroying the elves, their families, their lives, everything." She spread her arms wide. "The rail line is right on top of their homes. You have got to believe me and believe in them." Her flashing eyes grew wide.

---

[70] For all the good!

[71] Mother

"I do believe. And that, my little friend," he said friend as one would say enemy, "is the problem. I don't really believe it, but I see them with my own eyes. I have always seen them." He gestured towards Hoch and the others. "I remember Hoch, as you call him, from my school days. In fact, I remember a fat fellow who wore the most ridiculous outfits…" he paused to spit and his eyes were menacing.

"That would be Himmelwort and he hasn't changed a bit," laughed Penelope nervously, "except with the fashion." She continued to tell Herr Briefträger about the other elves, but when she mentioned Liedersinger, Herr Briefträger looked up sharply.

"I remember no such elf. Do not play with me, child." He scratched his chin. "I must relay all this to my mother. She will, I think, enjoy the story. However," Herr Briefträger looked down at Penelope with a scowl, "you have not mentioned *Schönelieberin*[72] or her ugly sister, *Regenbogen*[73]. Where are they? Do they not still…exist?" He said these names with a sneer and his small black eyes flashed.

"Who? I never heard the elves say those names." Penelope hoped he didn't see that she was a little scared of him now. Then she had a clear thought and ventured a guess. "You mentioned your mother. Is she the post lady?"

"*Doch!* [74] Who else would own the post office with a name like ours?" he added in a mocking voice.

"Briefträger, yes it means letter carrier. Why didn't I think of that? I suspected she knew something." Penelope nodded several times. A grown-up that believes in elves. There was

---

[72] Beautiful lover
[73] Rainbow
[74] Of course!

hope. She wanted to jump up and down, but the severe face of Herr Briefträger made her stop. Winning him over was not going well.

Out of the corner of her eye, Penelope noticed her teacher walking toward them. Frau Huybrechts' eyebrows were so scrunched together they cast a shadow across her face. Penelope stopped jumping and turned toward her.

"Miss Pond, I have looking everywhere for you. Where have you been? Please leave Herr Briefträger," she nodded at him, "alone. He has plenty to do without your interference. You must apologize and follow me at once to the bus."

Penelope was about to reply when Herr Briefträger spoke up, "*Genädige Frau, bitte*[75], you must accept my apologies for your...your eventful class trip." He coughed into his hand and continued. "My construction crew has been experiencing some, um... technical difficulties. However, I believe," he nodded at Penelope, "that all is under control now. Your Miss Pond has been most helpful. I trust your class had an interesting visit in any case." He turned to Penelope and forced a smile. "Miss Pond, if I can be of further assistance...with err...your project, you can reach me through the post, of course." He turned his gaze back to both of them and bowed slightly. "Thank you and I bid you *Auf Wiedersehen.*"

Penelope and her teacher had no time to answer as he had already walked off toward his office in a trailer on the site.

"*Komm jetzt*[76], we must hurry back to the school. *Wir sind so spät.*[77] We are quite behind schedule." Frau Huybrechts seemed

---

[75] Excuse me ma-am
[76] Come now
[77] We are so late

flustered and grabbed Penelope's arm and led her toward the waiting bus.

Penelope was so excited she could barely keep it to herself. She wanted to tell the kids on the bus about her adventure and her discovery about the construction chief. But when she boarded the bus, a group of kids started laughing and pointing at her yelling led by none other than the mean boy Marcus, who yelled out, "Look at miss high and mighty, probably asking for a job." Another voice piped up, "Yeah, bet he told her she was too tall!" Emily, whom Penelope considered her best friend until now, yelled, "I bet she was telling him about the little elf people hiding everywhere, ha ha ha." It sounded like the entire bus roared in agreement. Penelope sat down feeling a huge scream welling up inside her. She wanted to yell at them all, tell them they were wrong. SHE WAS RIGHT. Instead she turned, deep in thought, and gazed out the window, seeing nothing outside the window but knowing inside she was on the right track.

A Thank You Note

Amelia came running down the stairs as soon as she heard Penelope was home from school. "What happened at the construction site, Pel? Did you save the elves?" In her excitement she stepped on the cat's tail and Sammy let out a screech.

"Calm down, Amelia. Mom will hear you." Penelope peered about the house, and then turned to her sister. "You wouldn't believe what happened..." and she proceeded to make Amelia's eyes widen with her tales of elfin mischief.

"But what happens now, Pel? You didn't save the elves yet. Herr Briefträger believes, so what. And his mother probably is a real witch. I told you she looked like one. Did he promise to stop building the train line?"

"Not exactly." Penelope scrunched up her eyes, and twisted some hair. "But, he did say to contact him through the post. Come on. We've got a letter to write."

The girls scurried up to their room and hurriedly composed a note to the construction chief. Penelope read it aloud before sealing it.

> *Liebe Herr Briefträger,*
> I am so glad I met you today and that you understand the problem about the elves. I

know you will do the right thing and stop all the construction at once. The elves will be so happy.

Sincerely, Penelope Pond, friend of the elves.

"Can't I write my name too? I wanna help the elves and…" Amelia asked.

"Okay, okay. Here, sign your name." Penelope pointed.

And Amelia wrote in big letters at the bottom:

Amelia Pond, a real believer in elves!

The girls sealed the envelope marked 'Herr Briefträger' and plotted a visit to the post office, but were interrupted by Mom standing in the doorway.

"Homework time, everyone. Amelia, have you memorized your German words already?"

"Oh, hi Mom. Uh, yes. But I have to help Penelope mail this letter and then…"

"What letter? Can I see?" Mrs. Pond reached out her hand.

"It's nothing Mom. Just a letter to a friend at school," Penelope stuttered in a rush.

Her mom glanced at the envelope and stammered, "Herr Br…Brieftr…. Penelope? Who is this person? A MAN? Why are…"

Her mom's words were cut off by a crash downstairs. All three ran down to see what happened. They found a sheepish Tucker standing in the middle of the kitchen amidst a pile of broken glass.

"Tucker, honey, are you alright? Don't move. Let me clean up." As Mrs. Pond went to retrieve a dustpan, Tucker waved to his sisters and put a chubby finger to his lips. Then with a clumsy but obvious wink he pointed to the letter in Penelope's hand.

Penelope stared at it for a moment and then felt Amelia grab her arm and yank her out of the kitchen and toward the front door.

"Come on, dummy. Don't you get it? Tucker is helping us." Then, shaking her head, "Why in the world did the elves ever choose you to help them?" Amelia rolled her eyes and headed for the post office with a stunned Penelope in tow.

They found the post office quite busy and only managed to lay the envelope on the counter before it was quickly swept away by the post lady. Hexe gave them no sign of recognition. Feeling a bit deflated they trudged up the steep hill home.

A Troublesome Reply

One week passed. No letter came from the construction chief and more ominously, the post lady acted annoyed each time the girls entered the post office. Cold gray weather settled in around the *Taunus*[78] area signaling the advent of winter. Penelope and Amelia felt it seeping into their hearts. Silence beckoned from the woods, as there was no word either from the elves. The only good news the foul weather brought was the halt of construction, temporarily, on the rail line. The frozen earth prohibited more digging and high winds made cable lying too dangerous.

For Penelope, *Martinstag*[79] brought some much needed cheer. St. Martin's Day was a holiday celebrating the charitable goodness of the Roman soldier, Martin, who sliced his cloak and gave half to a beggar. The German villages commemorated the event with an evening parade of all the town's children carrying self-made lanterns as they followed St. Martin on a horse to the center of the village where a giant bonfire burned and crackled in the crisp air.

---

[78] The Taunus is a low mountain range north of Wiesbaden known for spas and fresh healing air.
[79] Saint Martin's Day, November 11

Penelope, Amelia and Tucker gathered around the fire with the rest of Eppstein's children and sang songs, each holding a lantern, their cheeks glowing red and orange as the flames pierced the night sky, spreading warmth and light.

"Lanterne, Lanterne, Sonn und Mond und Sterne…"[80] Penelope sang gaily later as they walked home still aglow from the late night fun. She fell asleep warm and happy and unaware that there was a note taped to her window next to her bed.

The morning sun brought little good cheer. As Penelope shook her self awake and gazed out her window, she spied the little note. It was not a reply from Herr Briefträger as she expected.

Penelope read the note:

Liebe süsse Mädchen,[81]

It is with great sadness that I write you this letter. Your courageous efforts to convince Herr Briefträger of our plight have lightened our hearts but, regretfully, have but hardened his. As I write, he is planning to increase his efforts with the construction and in doing so, hasten our destruction. We believe it is out of anger and misplaced jealousy from his past that he acts so cruelly. I must apologize, dear girl, for though you were able to convince him that we do exist as we always had in his mind, he is consumed with renewed hatred. He does indeed believe and it is out of revenge, not ignorance, that he builds the rail line now. I leave you now to make plans to evacuate. Never forget your friends the elves.

Yours forever, Hochsternigen

---

[80] Lanterns, lanterns, sun and moon and stars
[81] Dear sweet girls

"Oh-ma-gosh. No, it can't be." Penelope cried as she looked up from the letter. What had gone wrong with Herr Briefträger? He had acted a little weird but he had definitely believed. What was the problem? Did he know something more about the elves? Penelope ran to Amelia's room to show her the letter.

Amelia responded with panic in her voice, "Penelope, we have to stop them. The elves can't move anywhere else. They need the magic in that special spot to survive. They'll DIE if they move." She looked up at her sister with tears in her eyes.

"I know. Amelia, I know. Quick, let's bike over to the site now and stop the elves."

Amelia and Penelope grabbed their bikes from the shed and strapped on their helmets. Just then, a strange car pulled into the driveway. A tall woman carrying a briefcase got out of the car. At the same time, Mrs. Pond opened the door to the house.

"Penelope honey, I have someone here I want you to meet. She's been looking forward to meeting you ever since I mentioned your, um, your friends the elves. Her mom shrugged apologetically. "Honey, she is a children's psychologist and has agreed to talk to you and help you and…"

Penelope was in shock. Why now? Of all the times to have to meet a Doctor. Now what would happen to the elves? Her mom and this lady would never understand.

"Hi." It was all she could think of to say.

Doctor's Advice

"Guten Tag[82] and welcome, *Frau Doktor Kopffall.*[83] Let's go inside where you and Penelope will be more comfortable." Mrs. Pond glanced over at Penelope with a dark, but pleading expression to join them peacefully.

"Mom, but Amelia and I have something so important to do. We have to…"

"SAVE THE ELVES, MOM. RIGHT NOW!" yelled Amelia, eyes ablaze. "THEY ARE ABOUT TO DIE!"

"Well, Mrs. Pond. I see you have very interesting daughters. I look forward to talking with…both of them. Is this possible?"

"Of course, I mean, sure if you think it necessary. Really, it is Penelope who started this…whole thing and…"

"Come girls. I look forward to our chat." In a matter of minutes, Penelope, Dr. Kopffall and Amelia were all seated in the living room while Mrs. Pond made herself scarce.

"Tell me about yourselves, girls. Moving to Germany must have been quite a change for you both. It is quite different here, isn't it?"

Penelope could see where the Doctor was headed. She was going to probe them for information to see if they were

[82] Good day
[83] Dr. Head Accident

crazy or not. She had seen enough shows on TV to smell a rat. So, she decided to save time. She blurted out, "Amelia and I have made friends with elves who live in your country whether you know it or not. I'm sure you think we are making this up and that we are just homesick children but we're not. The elves are in trouble because of people like you who think everything has to make perfect sense and fit onto a computer disk. Amelia and I have no time to talk to you 'cause right now the elves are leaving before they get run over by bulldozers at the construction site for the new train to Cologne.[84] It is our last chance to save them." By now, Penelope was out of breath and quite upset.

Amelia piped in, looking brave and determined as well. "Penelope is right, Doctor Lady. They need our help 'cause we're kids and we believe. Only people who believe can help so that means you can't!" She sat back against the sofa, arms crossed.

"Girls, Penelope, Amelia. Please. It's okay. I am here to help. Believe or not, I am interested, now. You sound, well, believable," and she smiled.

Penelope looked over at Amelia and raised her eyebrows. She turned to the psychologist. "If you want to help, I've been thinking. Do you know who is in charge of the High-Speed rail-line that is being built through the woods here? I don't mean who is construction chief, either." She nodded to Amelia. "We already know him. I mean the head…"

"You mean, who is the government Minister of Transport? Is that your question?" She looked down at her lap where she

---

[84] Cologne (Köln) is a city along the Rhine River, about 80 miles north of Frankfurt

had been busy writing on a tablet. "I had no idea you were so, so serious. Yes, I believe I can get you his name."

"We also need his address so we can speak to him in private," added Penelope. "It is urgent. Also, it would be really great if you tell our mom we're not crazy or anything."

"Yeah," agreed Amelia. "Everyone thinks we are loony." She doubled over in giggles.

"Yes, I see. Well girls, I must speak to your mother for a bit. I am quite pleased we had a chance to talk and that you were kind enough to share your, um, troubles with me." I look forward to our next meeting. *Auf Wiedersehen.*"

The girls headed upstairs as their mother joined the psychologist in the living room. "We can listen to them from here," whispered Penelope as they crouched at the top banister.

"Such delightful, animated girls!" announced Frau Doctor Kopffall. "Rarely do I meet such engaging young people."

"Yes, well, thank you. But do you see my point. They are completely absorbed with this elf-thing."

"I agree. However, I have been thinking. Perhaps you are approaching the issue all wrong. Instead of disagreeing and challenging the girls on something they feel quite strongly about, I feel it may be more prudent to coach them through this, this delusion."

"Delooshun! What's a deloo…whatever, Penelope?" whispered Amelia.

"…so, you're saying, go along with them for a while?" questioned Mrs. Pond with obvious doubt in her voice.

"Exactly what I'm saying," soothed the Doctor. "Perhaps it will bring the delusion to a quicker and satisfactory end."

"I don't believe this!" gasped Penelope as she pulled her sister into their room. "The lady is a fake. She only pretended she wanted to help. Well, we'll show her."

"How?" asked Amelia.

"I don't know yet. Wait. Let's get that name and address from her for sure. I guess it is still only up to us 'delusioned' kids to save the elves."

A Short Visit

As the skies clouded over, Penelope and Amelia wasted no time in rushing to the elfin circle in the wood to stop Hoch and friends from evacuating. Mrs. Pond did not try to prevent them from "playing with the little elf-people" as she now termed their delusion.

"I hope we're not too late," panted Penelope as she pedaled looking over her shoulder at her sister, her breath bursting in steamy puffs in the chilly air, her bike tires crunching the nearly frozen earth.

What if they are gone, or even dead?" Amelia whispered this last word with dread.

"Don't even say THAT!" screamed Penelope as she hopped off her bike, leaving it twisted in a heap as she ran through the trees toward their last meeting place. The hard ground swallowed their footsteps. "Hoch! Mondwagen! Himmelwort! Where are you? Please, it's me, Penelope. Don't give up. I have another plan...I want..."

She stopped yelling. There, on all the stones in a circle, sat the elves. Fallen trees and dismembered limbs and branches littered the forest floor around them, evidence of the ongoing construction. Hoch began to speak in a solemn voice. As he did, large snowflakes fell from the sky.

"Dear child. The elfin people have made a decision. Like our distant cousins, the gnomes, we are going to leave your world. It is "your" world now: the world of human beings, technology and the relentless drive to destroy this earth. Your world leaves little room for imagination and fairy tales." He shook his head looking down. "This great earth is not big enough for elves and humans to live in harmony. Your species needs nothing from us. You have everything you need on computers, or you think you do! Your construction is our destruction." He scoffed and continued. "Our land here is sacred and cannot be replaced. The very source of our existence is the centuries old magic, found in the soil, the trees, and the air in these last elfin woods." He glanced upwards at the tall trees, which cast a long shadow over the faces of the other elves.

"But Hoch, wait." She began to jump up and down, but then thought better of it and continued in a calmer voice. "Please. Listen to my plan. I have an idea that will get to the source. I mean, I'm going to meet the head of the whole ICE[85] rail project and convince him to move the line. I can. We found out that Herr Briefträger was the wrong person." Penelope then paused at looked directly in to Hoch's solemn face.

"Hoch, what happened with Herr Briefträger anyway? In the past, I mean. Why does he hate you?" She stood tall with feet firmly apart and arms crossed looking quite determined. "I think that you haven't told me everything. Herr Briefträger already believed in elves and yet he was and still is your enemy. Why?"

---

[85] Inter City Express

Hoch raised his eyebrows dislodging a random snowflake that had landed there before answering. "Yes, I see we have some explaining to do here." He looked around at his fellow elves and nodded. "When Herr Briefträger was but a young lad of seventeen earth years, the elfin peoples contacted him. You see, we knew of our pending doom even then. We believed he could save us if we enlightened him early enough in his young life. We believed we could alter the future through him."

"You mean you thought if he believed in elves he would never build a rail line later when he grew up, or something like that?" guessed Penelope with wide eyes.

Hoch nodded and all the other elves murmured in agreement.

Sensing their embarrassment, Penelope said quietly, "Then what went wrong. I mean, it was a good idea and all..."

Hoch bowed at once to Penelope and said, "Forgive us, young and wise child; we have not been entirely true. We have left out a portion of the tale. You see, Herr Briefträger was to be our rescuer, our savior, if you will. Or at least we believed. We entrusted him with our elfin secrets and he too, like you, could see and speak with us in elfin tongue. For a long while he was our comrade." Hoch bowed his head. "If we had only listened to the prophecy, followed it to the letter, things would have never gotten out of hand."

"Why? What is this prophecy anyway? Where do I fit in Hoch?" prodded Penelope sounding older than her years.

Hoch looked Penelope straight in the eye. "Yes. You are right." He turned to his fellow elves and then turned once more to Penelope. The snow was falling steadier now in smaller flakes. "You see, the prophecy spoke of a youth who would appear at a time in our elfin world when we felt desperate…"

Hoch was interrupted by Mondwagen who pulled a small scroll out of his cloak, unrolled it with a flourish and said, clearing his throat with a dramatic 'ahem', "I believe the true elfin oracle bodes as follows:

> Elfin gyromancy is ever true
> Spiraling through time, cleft and hue
> Apocalyptic calamity is foreseeable
> Unless agreement of the Two"

Mondwagen looked up through his glasses at Penelope, "The oracle or prophecy is speaking of our magic and its ability to tell the future. It warns of a terrible, world-ending disaster if the Two don't agree. The Two being you and me. Man and Elf, so to speak," he said clearly as a teacher would to a child.

"But where does it say Penelope must save the elves? Sounds like any ol' person can do the job," interjected an ever-doubting Amelia, "including Herr Briefträger."

"Please allow me to finish. I was getting to that part, impatient one." Mondwagen looked down his nose casting a sideways glance at Amelia, and then down at the scroll, shook his head sending powdery puffs of snow everywhere including onto the precious scroll. Embarrassed, he wiped off this snow trying to appear important. His eyes darted about and then back to the scroll and he read aloud:

> "A time in space will come
> Data will be the Dictum
> Magic cast aside to die
> Salvation beats in a child's eye

Aren't you going to interrupt?" Mondwagen interrupted himself peering over at Amelia.

"No, I get it." Amelia retorted. "Data is like computer data, right? Except, what is a dicshun? I get the part about a child saving the day. That's easy." She winked at Penelope, who was silent in concentration, her long hair white with snowflakes.

"A dictum is an order of sorts, as in the law of the day. You know, what people follow," Mondwagen answered, obviously proud of himself.

Hoch raised his hand, "Enough, read the prophecy to the end."

Mondwagen bent his head down once more:

"Fair and tall, one among many
Forged wings bear him near
A loyal carrier of the heart
Water, is thy name

"So you see it becomes much more specific," Mondwagen looked up.

Amelia couldn't resist, "That's not very exact, that prophecy. Why did you think Herr Briefträger was…the one?"

Hoch answered. "Herr Briefträger came to us when he was a boy. It was really the beginning of the information age, some forty years ago. Technology was in, enlightenment of thought, was out. The elves were in trouble across the globe, although not as bad as we are in now," he swept his arms outward as if to show the turmoil. "Herr Briefträger, 'Klaus' we called him, stumbled upon a group of us when he crashed his model airplane. A tall boy with blond hair, and his name, Briefträger, means letter 'carrier'. The pieces all seemed to fit."

"What about the water part?" Amelia continued acting like an interrogator. Through the snowfall, Penelope could see Amelia pointing a finger at Hoch.

"We should have known to trust the prophecy in its entirety and to question this omission. This was our downfall." Hoch sighed and bowed his head.

Penelope awoke from her intense concentration and looked at Hoch. "I still wonder why you think it is me the prophecy's talking about. I mean, it says "him" in the last stanza and "Man" in the first. Okay, my last name is Pond. That must be the water part. I want to help but I want to be sure you've got the right person," she said with her eyes large and pleading.

"Earth child, it is you. A 'carrier of the heart' is a woman in our tongue. The females of our species are often represented by hearts, because they show their feelings and emotions more often than the males. I did not wish to acknowledge this doubt concerning Herr Briefträger. However, dear child, what's done is done. We shared too much with him. We will now share the full story with you and trust you are still willing to help us." Hoch paused dramatically. "Herr Briefträger became enamored with one of our elfin ladies fair." Here, Hoch paused and looked over at Liedersinger. "Come forward elf-maiden."

Liedersinger stepped into the center of the ring and in a silent flash, shed his outer garments. Underneath he was a she! Her outfit was spectacular, made of gold, glitter and silver. It was both feminine and warrior-like.

Penelope was struck dumb. Even though she suspected Liedersinger was female, the transformation was unbelievable. This elf was…well…beautiful. She had black hair nearly as long as the others' beards, but it was braided and hung down the back of her shimmering outfit. She was neither tall nor short, fat nor slim. Rather, she appeared perfect. The longer she stood before Penelope, calm and composed, the more fidgety Penelope became. 'Am I under some kind of spell?' she wondered.

Shaking her head as if to clear a fog, Penelope managed to ask in a croak, "Are you *Schoen...Schönelieberin* or...or...well, you can't be the ugly sister, right?" Penelope realized with a start that she had said this out loud. She turned bright red and started to apologize. "I am so sorry. I mean, he said she was ugly, not me and..."

Hoch saved her from further embarrassment. "Penelope! What do you know of Regenbogen, or her sister here?" He pointed at Liedersinger. "Answer child."

"I...I...I don't know her at all. It was Herr Briefträger who mentioned her. He seemed to know a lot about..." Penelope stuttered.

"He's going to KILL US ALL!" shrieked Mondwagen, who suddenly lost his earlier calm. "He tried to kill Regenbogen. He did. And now he will finish off us all..." Mondwagen's voice trailed off into a low wail, lost in the heavy snowfall.

"Kill Regenbogen? What are you talking about?" cried Penelope as she stared in horror at the elves. "What is going on?" She started to pace back and forth. "You ask me, me, a fourth grader, to help you. And then you keep all these terrible secrets from me. Well, you can just keep me out of it. I am going home. Come on Amelia!"

A Grim Tale

"Wait. Please." Hoch held up his hand. "I am truly sorry and apologize for withholding these facts. We did not wish to alarm you any more than we needed to. Ours is a grim tale." [86] He winked. "No pun intended."

"Well, if you could please fill me in, it would help," snapped Penelope.

"Yeah," chimed in Amelia. "How do you expect us to solve your problem when we don't have the facts?" She smacked her hands together.

Hoch looked up to the trees as if looking for an answer, but the falling snow forced him to look back down, and he explained, "The entire affair started when Herr Briefträger was introduced to Schönelieberin. The pair was never supposed to meet. Herr Briefträger fell immediately in love with Schönelieberin. She never returned his love." He glanced over at the elf maiden who was standing poised and still. "You see, Schönelieberin, her real name, has a spell cast upon her that makes her irresistible to others and they cannot help but desire her. Normally we keep her hidden from humans.

---

[86] Referring to the brothers Grimm, who compiled the *"Haus-Märchen"*, fairy tales

84

Herr Briefträger fell under her spell and could not bear life without her. He followed her, stalked her. She became afraid of him." Hoch shook his head, his beard shook as well. "Most unfortunate," he muttered.

"It was worse for her sister," interrupted Mondwagen sobbing. "She got in his way, so he plotted the end of our Rainbow."

Penelope must have appeared confused for Schönelieberin spoke up. Her voice as soft as velvet, "Regenbogen is aptly named. It translates from German as rainbow in your language. You see, on the day of her birth, the largest rainbow in our luscious rainforest land, filled the morning sky. Our people, the Rain Forest Elves, interpreted it as a sign that Regenbogen would bring peace and light back to the troubled elfin peoples." A tiny sob escaped her lips. "Little did we know that even after escaping the destruction and desecration of the rainforest, she would meet her end so soon and in such a foul and useless manner? She never had the chance to save us."

Hoch was pacing back and forth. The snow underfoot was soft and silent. He stopped and looked into all the elves eyes, one by one. "Herr Briefträger did not kill her, friends. I know. You must trust me for now." Hoch turned to Penelope. "You see, Regenbogen was never found. Herr Briefträger was the last one seen with her. Naturally, we banished him from our kingdom and forbade him ever to contact the elves again. Many powerful charms kept him away, and over time, his heart hardened and he believed less and less in the existence of elves."

"But I thought he was in love with Schönelieberin, not Regenbogen. Why did he bother about her, the rainbow one?

And why then," continued a baffled Penelope, shaking her head, "did you ever want me to convince Herr Briefträger again, of your existence? Doesn't seem like a very good idea, if he was so dangerous?"

"It was my idea." Everyone fell silent with the caressing words of Schönelieberin. "I believed there was some good in him. After all it was not his fault he fell under my spell. I felt, well, responsible." She hung her beautiful head. "I still do." She looked back up at Penelope with tears in her eyes. "My sister was very dear to me. I'm sure as your sister," she glanced at Amelia, "is dear to you."

Amelia shrugged her shoulders with an impish grin.

Schönelieberin continued, "I had hoped Hans Briefträger could tell me what has become of Regenbogen." Now, she turned her powerful stare on Hoch.

Hoch continued, "I agreed with her because we needed him in his high position. With his power over the construction line, we were at his mercy. Or so we thought." Hoch shook his head in disgust. "We believed he would act in a fair and just manner, and save the people for whom he once cared deeply."

"Boy, are you guys ever trusting," quipped Amelia.

"Yes, and for this trust, I have placed the elfin people in even greater peril. I believe now that Herr Briefträger will stop at nothing to build this rail line and…" Hoch looked away.

"RUN US OVER WITH THE FIRST TRAIN," screamed a now hysterical Mondwagen.

"Therefore, we have to go to the top, to someone who can be convinced the right way at once," interrupted Penelope in a firm voice. She picked up a large twig and held it high in the air. "And I need your help to do it. Together we can stop the line and save you all. However," she turned and like Hoch, looked at all the elves one by one, "you have to promise me that you won't keep any more secrets from me." She stopped at Schönelieberin. "Maybe you should keep up your disguise as Liedersinger. It might be safer," she added with a smile, and then continued. "I will try and open the hard human hearts and you must show your trusting ways. I know we can all live together on this land peacefully. We must."

"Yes, you people have to believe her," pleaded Amelia, stepping forward, "cause that 'ole prophecy said you guys would be saved? Huh?" She glared at the elves with crossed arms and a tapping foot.

"By a Leprechaun's whiskers, she's right," blurted out Himmelwort. "We shall succeed, or else, humans will never know about the elves. I certainly don't want to be confused with a sneaky Leprechaun who's always tricking gullible humans. Humans will confuse us with Leprechauns, I know it." He paused for a moment, "though I do like their little hats."

"No, Himmelwort. You will be remembered as the fattest, most ridiculously dressed elf that ever lived in these woods!" added Mondwagen, trying not to smile.

Indeed, Himmelwort did appear rather strangely dressed. He wore a long green cloak. One could see a bright red and white striped outfit, like pajamas, underneath. Only on Himmelwort the Large, they were skin-tight. Hanging from his cloak were hundreds of tiny watches. Some were wristwatches, some were pocket watches. Most were gold or silver but here and there hung a brightly colored plastic watch.

"This was a typical elfin costume from the Fourth Dynasty, I'll have you know. I respect the traditions of my elders and wish to depart in style." He said in a huff.

"Yes, but why the watches, dear friend?" asked Mondwagen. "Don't want to be late for your own funeral, do you." With this statement, Mondwagen burst into tears and began wailing uncontrollably. The sobs were absorbed by the snow.

"Oh stop your blubbering, Mondwagen. I merely wanted to display my human treasures that I have collected over the years here in these woods. Humans are the most careless people I have ever met. Just check out this Snow White and the Seven Gnomes watch. The real Gnomes would just die laughing. Look, see the beards. Those are elfin beards. And the axes. As if Gnomes ever did any honest day's work in their lives."

Himmelwort's laughter was contagious and soon the entire circle rocked with laughter. Hoch's familiar raised hand gesture calmed down everyone. He looked over at Penelope and her sister, and smiled.

"As you say in your world, 'this is our last chance'. We will allow you to try this last time to save the elfin people here from complete extinction. If elfin prophecy is to hold true, it is beyond our powers to thwart it. So we must trust a human once more and risk our very lives."

Hoch stood and bowed to Penelope and then to Amelia. "Now, please tell us of your plan," and he winked, "and how we can help."

Penelope looked over at her sister and then at the elves who were gazing at her like she was a pot of gold or something. She took one big swallow and told them of her plan. The elves nodded and grinned. Even the once again transformed Liedersinger jumped up and down with excitement.

"This will work. This will work. Okay, next week then." They all hummed and whispered. As if by magic, the falling snow stopped and the forest was clear. Trees and ground were illuminated in soft white light.

"What shall I wear?" asked Himmelwort with great seriousness.

A Christmas Present

"With all this lovely snow on the ground I think it would a great time to visit the *"Weihnachtsmarkt?"*[87] Mrs. Pond suggested as she pulled aside the white curtains and gazed out the front window. "It certainly looks magical out there," she smiled.

"Oh yes, let's go to the Christmas Market. They have hot chocolate and sugary pretzels and toys and stuff," Amelia added pumping her arm in the air. "Lexi said so. I'm ready. Come on Penelope," she said in an excited rush. "Grab Tucker from Lego land and let's go!" Laughing at her own joke, Amelia ripped her coat from the hook and was out the door.

Mrs. Pond turned toward the slamming door. "I guess there's no time like the present," she smiled and went into the hall to unhook her coat from the still wobbling coat tree silently wishing German houses had more closets.

The *Weihnachtsmarkt* was set up as a cozy fair in the center of the *Altstadt.* Snow-covered small wooden booths were scattered about, each decorated with red and green garlands and twinkling white lights. Handmade goods and sweet smelling goodies were on display and tempted the bundled up passerby. A trio singing Christmas carols warmed the brisk night air.

---

[87] Christmas Fair

"What is *Glühwein*?"[88] Asked Penelope with eyebrows raised after reading a painted sign above a steamy stall. "The Germans put *glue* in their wine? Yuck," she laughed. Her eyes darted eagerly to the next stall where a red-faced man was dipping large soft pretzels into sugar. "Oh yum…Tucker, Amelia, here are the sugary pretzels!"

She turned to see Tucker in a starry-eyed trance. A booth filled with colorful hand-carved trains had his complete attention. Smoke, from a nearby incense-seller, stung her eyes.

Amelia, holding a porcelain mug of hot chocolate turned to see and BANG. She bumped into a woman, spilling her hot drink into the white snow. Mouth open, she watched it steam and evaporate into a brown blotch. She mumbled a small "I'm sorry."

"*Oopsala Kinder, es macht nichts.*"[89] A familiar voice rang out politely.

"Frau Doctor Kopffall?" Amelia looked up at the woman. "What are you doing here?"

"Amelia, don't be rude. Everyone comes to the *Weihnachtsmarkt*. It's Christmastime silly." Penelope added looking to make sure the doctor lady was not angry.

"*Guten Abend*[90] to the both of you. Amelia, let me replace your cup of *heisse Schokolade*?"[91] With that she grabbed Amelia and Penelopes' arms in hers and walked toward the steaming hot chocolate booth, chatting all the way.

Later they all met up with Mrs. Pond and Tucker who was humming and holding a small, red-painted train caboose. "It

---

[88] Mulled or spiced red wine
[89] Oops, children, it's nothing
[90] Good Evening
[91] Hot Chocolate

was so nice to chat with you both. Penelope, I find you and your sister so interesting. I feel honored to be a member of your elf, shall we say, circle." Frau Kopffall was all smiles and winks. "Oh, before I forget, here is that name and address you requested. I am so happy to be of help."

"Yeah, well thanks and…Auf," Amelia snatched the paper from the psychologist's hand, "Wiedersehen."

Penelope was more polite with a merry *"Frohe Weihnachten"*[92]as she nodded goodbye. Once they saw Frau Kopffall leave, walking around a large steaming metal barrel in which a man was roasting and selling chestnuts, she and Amelia scanned the note in the light of the fire.

"Where is the *Messeturm*[93] in Frankfurt? What is the *Messe*" mumbled Amelia. "I don't like the sound of it." She crinkled her nose and frowned. "Frau Kopffall could be tricking us. She was way too nice tonight, buying me *two* hot chocolates with whipped cream."

"Oh Amelia, don't be so doubting. She just wants to cure us of our elf-delusion, not hurt us. Let's ask Dad about this "Messy" place. We can ask him tonight to show us on a map." Penelope smiled, "This is great. Don't you see? With this address and name," she waved the scrap of paper gleefully, "We can help the elves for real!"

"How will we get there? I'm not going on the *S-Bahn*[94]alone with only you. I'd be too scared."

"What if the elves came along? Would you still be scared?"

---

[92] Merry Christmas
[93] The Trade Tower
[94] Strassenbahn or local train

Train Travel

Two days later, Penelope and Amelia huddled together on a seat on the S-2 to Frankfurt. Sitting across from them sat their stern-faced mother, who kept rubbing her hands together and rolling her eyes like she was nervous.

"I can't believe I am accompanying you on this wild goose chase," she scowled. "I have a good mind to tell Dr. Kopffall what I think of her 'go-along-with-this-elf-thing' attitude. Now, I am traveling to Frankfurt on a perfectly nice day to help you children," she emphasized this last word, "convince a German Government Minister of the existence of elves!" With this last word, she slumped back against the seat and stared out the window, shaking her head.

Amelia whispered to her sister as she eyed her mom with a worried look, "You said the elves would go with us, Pel. Where are they? Huh?" Amelia threw up her arms.

"Don't worry. They'll show," Penelope answered although she too was a bit worried. Hoch promised he would join them on the train. She looked over at her mother. "Mom, really, it's okay. I promise we are not crazy. You won't be embarrassed. You might even see an elf if you try to believe." She looked about the sparsely populated car.

"Look, over there! Is that man an elf, or what?" shouted Amelia.

"Amelia that is an old lady. Shh, don't be rude," cautioned her big sister.

A couple of seconds later a door opened at the end of the train car, and the *Bahn's* ticket-taker came in and started checking people's tickets. Right behind him, mimicking his brusque style walked Himmelwort. True to form, the elf was dressed, well, stylishly. He wore a train conductor's uniform, decorated with epaulets and brass buttons. He would have been quite convincing if only he weren't so short, and so hairy. His head barely cleared the top of the seats.

"Tickets please, ladies," he said and winked conspiratorially at Amelia and Penelope. The other passengers could not see him and stared vacantly from their seats.

"Oh, Himmelwort, you are so funny," squealed the girls with glee. "Where are the others?"

"Why, driving the train, of course. We elves are quite experienced at many things. Please disembark at station, *Taunusanlage*,[95] thank you. By the way, pay attention to your mother." Then, he walked on to the next car.

The sisters looked at one another and then at their mother and then rolled their eyes at the same time. Mrs. Pond's face was beet-red as she asked, "Who are you talking to? Everyone is staring at us."

Sure enough, all the passengers were now indeed staring and mumbling.

---

[95] Taunus passage, a park area

"Himmelwort, Mom. He is so silly," giggled Amelia. "Oh, and guess who is driving the train? Huh?" She bounced up and down on the seat.

"This is simply too much. I am taking you girls home." She stood as if to leave the train, which was still speeding down the track toward Frankfurt. The dark green valleys and curvy track through the countryside gave way to heavily populated areas, industrial parks, and train yards and then in a whoosh, the *S-Bahn* went underground.

Penelope saw that they were getting close. "Mom, no, really. Just let us do this one thing, and we'll never ever mention elves again," she added with both hands pleading in prayer form.

"Yes, pretty-please, Mom, I swear," Amelia crossed her hands over her heart and looked at her mom with big teary brown eyes.

"Well, against my better judgment, I will go on. But not another word about elves after this." She looked both daughters in the eye and appeared quite pleased with herself.

"*Nächste Haltestelle, Taunusanlage*"[96] crackled the loud speaker.

"Hey, that's Mondwagen's voice," cried Amelia. He must be our driver." The girls almost fell over as the train came to a screeching halt. Many passengers were angry and mumbling about the driver's skills.

"Quick, get off before they close the doors, girls," urged their mom as they hurried off the train. However, there was no need to rush, for the train remained where it was and did not leave. Penelope spied Mondwagen leaving the driver's cab

---

[96] Next stop Taunus Passage

with a big grin on his face. An announcement soon followed explaining that the train would not continue.

Standing on the station platform, Penelope and Amelia burst out laughing. Their mother looked at them with a puzzled expression and raised her eyebrows. She hastily scanned the area for an exit sign.

"This way Mom. It says the *Ausgang*[97] for *Messe* is over here," pointed Penelope.

---

[97] Exit for pedestrians

A Tall Visit

Minutes later they were in the lobby of the towering pyramid-shaped-top skyscraper. A large wall plaque listed the names of businesses and their floor number. Several banks of elevators stood at the ready.

"What's her name again, Penelope?" asked Amelia as she craned her neck looking at the tall list.

"Here it is," exclaimed Penelope. "*Frau Glauberin*[98] *und*… Okay, let's go…hum…to the…Does that say the *elventh* floor?" Wide-eyed, Penelope turned to her mom and Amelia.

"No, dummy, it says the e-lev-enth floor," stuttered Amelia as she read and turned to Penelope with a lop-sided grin. "But I'd say it's a good sign."

A set of elevator doors opened and to the girls' surprise, Himmelwort greeted them for the second time that morning. Only this time he had adjusted his outfit to appear as a doorman. Gone were the epaulets and stripes on the sleeves, replaced by a round bellman's cap. His uniform did look convincing and they laughed.

Mrs. Pond stood in the corner and shook her head as her daughters laughed and cavorted with thin air.

"Where are the others?" asked Penelope.

---

[98] Ms. Believer

"You will see, my dear," whispered Himmelwort with a sparkle in his eye.

All four got off on the eleventh floor and gazed about at the plush and richly decorated set of offices. The walls were a dark wood, like mahogany, and held many impressive paintings of old men. Covering the highly polished floor were beautiful oriental rugs in rich, red hues. In front of them stretched a desk that was so long and high, Himmelwort was not able to see over it.

Behind this grand desk sat a solemn-faced woman who was dressed in a black suit with a red scarf. She matches the surroundings, thought Penelope. She glanced at the nameplate on the desk: *Frau Steinaugen*[99]. 'That's a good name for her,' thought Penelope, 'Stone eyes.'

"She looks mean," Amelia said in a whisper.

The stony-eyed woman looked up and then down at the trio before her. She dropped her head to peer at them over her red-rimmed eye glasses. "*Ihr müsst die Amerikanerinnen sein. Sollen wir Englisch oder Deutsch sprechen?*" [100] She asked and then lifted her chin waiting for a reply.

"*Englisch, bitte,*" answered Penelope to her mother's surprise.

Well, then. I *velcome* you. Frau *Glauberin* is expecting you." She nodded and smiled at Mrs. Pond who smiled back and looked quite relieved. "I *vill* contact her for you immediately," and she pushed a button on her vast desk. "She *vill* be right *vit* you."

Penelope looked around hoping to see Hoch or one of the elves. She felt nervous and unsure of herself all of a sudden.

---

[99] Ms. Stone eyes
[100] You must be the Americans. Shall we speak English or German?

Her shoulders started their customary slouching and she began twirling strands of hair. How could she, poor little Penelope, make this important lady believe? Maybe their plan was doomed from the start? As she was starting to twist her hair into knots, a door down the hall opened and out walked another woman.

Where the secretary was tall and thin, this lady was short and well, wide. She waddled down the hall and was all smiles. To accentuate her more than ample body, she wore a bright pink peasant-style dress with a white frilly apron tied around her round waist. Her blouse was white too with large puffy short sleeves.[101] Her whole attire clashed with the office décor. Around her neck, Penelope noticed a large silver locket that hung nearly to her waist. It swung like a pendulum as she walked.

When she finally reached them, Penelope saw that she was quite short. In fact, she was exactly the same height as Penelope. Suddenly, she felt a quick jab in her ribs. She glared at Amelia and started to say something when she saw what Amelia was trying to tell her.

Himmelwort was gazing at this lady with limpid eyes and obvious adoration. She would have fallen down laughing but the woman was speaking…to her.

"You must be the mysterious Penelope Pond," she exclaimed as she grasped both of Penelope's hands in hers. "Michaela Glauberin. I feel honored that you wish to bring your momentous problem to me." With this, she looked over at Mrs. Pond. "Your daughter is quite the politician. You should be proud of her. It is not often that I am approached by…um… the younger generation. My work is often quite dull and I

---

[101] A Dirndl is a traditional peasant costume dress with an apron

welcome your interesting visit. Needless to say, I have spoken with your…oh…that nice lady, Frau Kopffall, I believe. I hope I can be of service, dear child," she smiled at Penelope.

Penelope's mind was in a whirl. This lady seemed so genuine, and her eyes had such a nice twinkle. But she had spoken with Frau Kopffall, the traitor. The psychologist probably had already told her that Penelope's problem was all in her head. That she was merely a homesick ten-year old girl. What could she say now? She did manage a wobbly smile and shrugged her shoulders.

Frau Glauberin went on talking, "Well now. I believe we need some privacy. Shall we go into the conference room? These offices are so nice. Normally I work in an old-fashioned office at the *Hessischen Landtag*[102] in Wiesbaden[103], but I am here this week. Lucky me," and she chuckled. "Penelope and you-must-be-Amelia, please follow me." She looked over at an awe-struck Mrs. Pond. "Would you care to join us, Mrs. Pond? I leave it up to you."

Mrs. Pond nodded and hurriedly gathered her handbag and followed the comical-looking lady who had ushered away her daughters.

Penelope and Amelia looked at one another, shrugged their shoulders, and followed the pink lady down the hall. Amelia couldn't resist mimicking the woman's walk and waddled like her until Penelope elbowed her in the ribs to stop.

They entered a large bright room with an incredible view. Through huge sparkling panes of glass, the girls could see the city of Frankfurt above and below them. They gazed in awe at

---

[102]Hessen Parliament. Hessen is a state within Germany.
[103]Wiesbaden is the capitol of Hessen

the tall steel buildings, like trees in a forest growing around them. Amelia went over to the windows and looked upwards to the tops of nearby skyscrapers and down to the busy street below. "Wow, this is so cool. I wish Daddy could work here."

"It is quite impressive, isn't it?" Frau Glauberin said as she stood smiling at the girls. "I still get goose-bumps every time I come in here." She let the girls continue looking around for a while. Then she said, "Now, why don't we get down to business. You have a…um… problem," she paused, "and you want me to fix it. Am I correct?" She sat down in one of the leather swivel chairs at the giant conference table.

"Well, um, yes, you see…" Penelope didn't know where to begin.

Amelia did. She stood directly in front of the pink lady and said in a rush, "The fast train, you call it the ICE cube train or something. It is gonna run over the top of them and so they can't live there, so you have to stop it. They are DYING!" She added, eyes blazing.

Frau Glauberin raised her hand. "*Doch, doch,* please slow down, Amelia. You are going much too fast for my ears."

"I can explain," interrupted Penelope with a serious expression on her face. She looked about the room as if for help. She was actually looking for the elves. Where did Himmelwort go? Hoch promised he himself would come to. It was part of the plan. Nervous and not just a little scared, she turned back to the woman. "It all started last summer when we moved to Germany. Everything was fine, I mean, nothing was wrong. I knew we had to move and I was okay. I knew I would miss my friends and all, especially Allyson, but you see I expected that. What I didn't expect was, was…elves!" She blurted this last word out and raised her arms into the air.

As if summoned, and perfectly on cue, the door to the conference room opened and in walked Himmelwort.

"Hello, who is it?" asked Frau Glauberin expecting someone to enter the open doorway. It was obvious she did not see the elf.

Himmelwort was not easy to miss Penelope and Amelia noted. He was dressed like a medieval knight, in shining armor no less. The only thing missing was his steed. He clinked and clanked as he strode across the room. If armor can be skin-tight, this was. They couldn't see his face, covered by the metal helmet, but they could feel his big smile.

"Himmelwort!" they both cried out.

"*Himmel-who?*" Frau Glauberin asked in wonder at the outburst.

"Why, it's our friend, Himmelwort, the elf." they answered matter-of-factly.

"Oh, the elf. Of course." She turned toward the direction the girls were facing, "Hello Himmelwort. I am pleased to make your acquaintance."

"No, no. He's over there." Amelia pointed at him as he made his way, clanging and banging, to the windows.

"Yes, yes, of course. You girls must help an old lady." She motioned to Mrs. Pond who was examining the view. "Do you see the…the…the dear little man?" she stuttered.

"No I most certainly do not!" snorted Mrs. Pond, but she added, trying to smile. "Obviously my daughters do and I am supporting them in their...their search," she also stuttered.

"Well, I am prepared to help. It is my job as a civil servant, an elected official, an officer of the land, if you will. I promise to…"Frau Glauberin awkwardly tried regaining control.

Himmelwort spared them anymore political talk by tripping and crashing to the floor with a tremendous boom. The entire room shuddered and everyone stopped talking.

"What was that?" exclaimed Frau Glauberin with raised eyebrows. "It felt like an earthquake."

"More like a sonic boom," added Mrs. Pond craning her neck to look upwards and out the window as if searching for a plane.

Amelia and Penelope rushed to Himmelwort's aide and tried without success to upright the metal-laden elf.

"He is too heavy, Pel. He weighs a ton." Amelia lifted until she was red in the face.

"We need some help here." Penelope called to the two perplexed adults. She motioned for her Mom and Frau Glauberin to lend assistance.

"What? Help where? What are you talking about?" snapped her mom. "Penelope Pond, this is going too far…"

"Now, now, child, how can I help?" soothed the pink politician. Penelope could hear no sarcasm in her pleasant voice so she conceded.

"Here, lift under here." She grabbed Himmelwort by the armpits. "And pull really hard."

As if in answer to her call for help, the door to the room swung open and Hoch, Liedersinger, and Mondwagen entered the room in one great swagger. Mondwagen began at once to make fun of Himmelwort's predicament. "Some knight in shining armor, you are. How did you manage to fall when you don't even have a horse to fall off *of*?" His high, whining laughter echoed throughout the conference room.

Hoch raised his hand and began to speak in a calm manner. "It is obvious the ways of this highly technical society do not conform to elfin ways." He looked down at the unfortunate form of Himmelwort lying spread eagle upon the floor. He raised his bushy eyebrows and looked crosswise at Penelope who, along with a puffing Frau Glauberin, was sprawled on the floor at Himmelwort's side.

Something in the tone of his voice annoyed Penelope. She stood up to full height and faced Hoch with fire in her eyes. "Listen Hoch. Here we are, at the very place we need to be. Frau Glauberin, here," she pointed, "is trying very hard to believe, I believe," she added. "And as for our 'high-tech' society and your 'elf one' getting along, I think they could both learn a lot from each other." She gestured at Himmelwort. "He can't help it if he is clumsy. He means well and he is certainly more accepting of human ways than all of you. You say you want to get along and live 'in harmony', but do you? You scoff at all our advances, like computers and yes, even trains. And yet you really don't understand us at all. These things can be good. Humans can be good."

She shook her head. She was running out of breath. "What more can I do? I know I'm a child to you, but I know what is right." She pointed at Hoch and the elves, "I know you should be more accepting and tolerant of humans if you want to get along. Maybe buy a computer, I don't know. And you too," she pointed at her mother and Frau Glauberin. "Why can't you just trust me… and your own hearts and see? Believe in the magic of elves. It won't hurt you. You'll see. Think back to when you were a child. Wasn't it fun to believe in…well, everything? To play make-believe?" She looked at her mother with hands on her hips.

"Go, Penelope, go!" cheered Amelia, clambering onto the conference table.

Hoch nodded, "You are right, I believe now more than before in the prophecy. I believe in you, Penelope, champion of the elves." He started to apologize further.

In all the raucous, no one noticed Liedersinger had become still as a statue. She was staring at the pair still on the floor. Frau Glauberin was still trying to lift an unseen Himmelwort to his feet.

"My, is he ever heavy, and believe me, I know what it's like to be a bit overweight," she indicated her girth with a grin. Then after a second or two, she screamed.

"Wait a minute, I can feel him. *Mein Gott!*[104] There *is* something here." She dropped Himmelwort and fell back herself.

Penelope rushed to her aide. She fanned the woman's face with her hand and whispered to her, "I knew you'd believe. It's okay. He is a very nice elf and…"

Penelope's mother also rushed over to help Frau Glauberin. "Penelope, see what you have done. She's fainted. What are we going to do? We've got to call an ambulance." Then, she panicked to Amelia. "Amelia, what is the German 911?"

"Mom, don't worry," answered Amelia in a very grown-up voice. "It's always a bit like this when you see an elf for the first time."

---

[104]My God!

A Rainbow Appears

Frau Glauberin coughed and clutched her hand to her heart as she slowly opened her eyes. Penelope was gazing down at her but noticed that Frau Glauberin's eyes were not meeting hers. They were gazing with a cloudy look at someone next to her. Penelope looked to her left and saw Himmelwort propping himself up on one elbow. He too, was gazing into the blue twinkling eyes of Frau Glauberin. The pair appeared lost in a trance.

The softened air was shattered by a wail that arose from the lips of Liedersinger, now transformed once more into the glowing Schönelieberin. She had been staring at Frau Glauberin the entire time and now was brimming with a discovery.

"Meine liebste Schwester!" Du bist es!"[105] She cried and pointed as sparkling tears poured down her cheeks. "There is her silver locket. Regenbogen is found." With these words, she ran to Frau Glauberin and hugged her, kissing her cheeks one then the other.

Frau Glauberin, Penelope could see, nearly fainted a second time. There was a brief hesitation in her eyes, then a flicker of understanding as she clasped her hand around her locket and

---

[105]My beloved sister! It is you!

then she melted before their eyes. Penelope could see years of doubt fall away from her as she realized who and what she was.

"Wait a minute. What's going on here, Pel?" asked Amelia, who by now was used to being part of the action. "Who is Frau Glauberin? An elf? No way."

"Amelia, don't you see? She must be the missing sister, Regenbogen." She twisted her hair and thought aloud, "Only I don't understand why *she* didn't know it all along."

"Yeah, how could she *not* know she was an elf?" piped in a doubting Amelia with her hands on her hips.

Hoch, who had remained silent, now spoke up. "It is the elfin Charm of Protection. I suspected this was the case but I didn't want to mention it for fear of giving dear Schönelieberin any false hope.

"Why not? She would have liked to know that her sister was okay," stated Amelia in a know-it-all manner.

"Dear child," Hoch gave her a stern glance, "you are not versed in all the ways of elves. The Protection Charm is our most powerful and dangerous charm. It allows the user to forget and forgo his or her present and past life. It is used only when this life is in such grave and mortal danger that there is no other escape.

"What does it do, Hoch?" asked Penelope and she saw by the looks on their faces that everyone else in the room was asking the same question.

"Regenbogen was, at the very moment she called upon the charm, changed into someone else. In her case, it happened to be a human, this Frau Glauberin. Only," he paused for effect and gazed around the room, "she was not to know of the change. This is the power and the danger of the charm. One sacrifices his or her life, never to know who or what he or she will become. It is a bit frightening, indeed."

"It sounds worse than that, like death or something," mumbled Penelope. "I mean, she never knew who she really was."

Everyone turned and stared when Frau Glauberin-Regenbogen started to speak, "I did know who I was, deep down, that is. I always had a feeling I was someone else, someone more than Frau Glauberin, Government Minister of Transportation. When you spoke to me, Penelope, about your elfin problem, I knew I had to see you, to help in some way. So you see, all memory is not lost in the charm." She smiled and turned to her sister.

"Schönelieberin, how you must have worried? I had to leave you. That evil Briefträger thought I would be afraid of him and lead him to you. He threatened to kill me if I didn't help him. He was crazy. The charm was *our* escape, you see. Do not be sad. It was not such a bad life to be a human."

"What do you mean…life? How long have you been a human and not Regenbogen?" asked a confused Penelope.

"Oh, child, elves live great long lives. Beautiful Schönelieberin here is over one hundred earth years old. As Frau Glauberin, I am a…a mature woman of fifty five earth years," she winked. I have been Frau Glauberin for her entire life. Before that, I was a young elf maiden," she looked at Himmelwort with a sly grin, "with many suitors."

"How come you can remember now? I thought this, this charm was like forever?" asked Amelia, arms crossed and head cocked to one side.

"Penelope, here, broke the charm with her passion to make elves and humans see the errors of their ways. She joined the two worlds into one. Without her, I would have never been in contact with the elves. She became the bridge between the two cultures. You see," Frau Glauberin explained, "After speaking with Frau Kopffall from the school, I knew I had to meet this Penelope." she nodded at Penelope. "Frau Kopffall kept saying how convincing and passionate Penelope was about her belief in elves. Elves! It triggered something in me. I felt compelled to meet this girl. And now having done so, Penelope has forced me to remember my youth. I, as a human, feel the pull into the elfin world once more and", she gazed upwards into Schönelieberin's and then her eyes moved toward Himmelwort's face, "I felt love pulling me back."

At this point, Himmelwort, feeling very much the center of attention, cleared his throat and attempted to speak. However, the effort caused his steel helmet to slam shut, and his voice came out a muffled cry for help. Everyone couldn't help laughing.

Only Schönelieberin didn't join in. She asked her sister, "Why do you not again assume the form of Regenbogen? I see her only in your eyes and your ways."

Hoch answered for Regenbogen. "She can never again assume the body of Regenbogen. It is lost to the charm. It is enough that we have retrieved her, her elfin essence."

With these words, Mondwagen, looked up at Hoch and started to say something but was immediately silenced with a look from Hoch.

"Oh, yes, yes, it is wonderful to have even this much of Regenbogen back!" cried Schönelieberin. "I only wondered and…"

"And I for one am happy she looks the way she does!" boomed in Himmelwort as he had finally managed to shed his steel helmet. "We make a stunning pair, do we not? We will set all the fashion trends, in your world and ours."

While Penelope joined in the laughter, she remembered her mother. What was *she* thinking? She spun about searching for her mom but she needn't have worried. Her mom was lying flat on the floor with her hand being caressed by none other than Mondwagen. Her head was rocking back and forth and she was moaning, but she was okay. Penelope guessed she was probably trying not to see and believe the real scene happening before her.

Elves! She had done it. Frau Glauberin was convinced. How could she not? She turned out *to be an elf.* Who would have guessed? And falling in love with Himmelwort? How cute! Penelope's daydreaming was interrupted by an urgent cry from Amelia.

"So everybody's happy, now. What about tomorrow when the high-speed train flattens your whole community? I mean it's nice you found your sister and all…" she looked over at Schönelieberin and Frau Glauberin, "but what about the problem?"

Revenge of the Elf-Maidens

"She's right." Mondwagen stood up, dropping the still semi-conscious Mrs. Pond's hand with a thud. "We must stop the ICE train, otherwise all is for nothing. He turned back to the prone Mrs. Pond and knelt at her side, clasping her hand in both of his, "Fear not, mere mortal, I shall return to protect thee …or die in the attempt." He bowed his head and began to sob.

"PENELOPE! Who is this ridiculous creature? Get him away from me. At once! Girls, help me up. This is simply too…"

"In a minute, Mom. We have a big problem right now," Amelia looked to Hoch. "So what do we do, fire Herr Briefträger or something?"

"*Doch!*" cried an excited Frau Glauberin. "*Natürlich,*[106] we remove the evil man from his chief-engineer position and make sure he never works near the elves again. In fact, I'll make sure he never again works on land in Germany. After all," she smiled sweetly, "being a Government Minister does have its perks. I think, perhaps, he would enjoy a position on an oil rig in the North Sea!"

"In winter!" added a gleeful Schönelieberin.

---

[106]Naturally

Everyone clapped and cheered as Hoch and Mondwagen hoisted Frau Glauberin and Himmelwort to their feet. Standing side by side, they did indeed make a striking, if rather large, pair.

Penelope was already thinking ahead, "But, can you…um… move the rail lines? You see it already cuts right across the elfin homes and land. It is destroying their magic…and yours." Penelope asked in a small voice. "Is it too late?"

"Um, I see your point. Moving the already laid tracks? A great deal of time, money and effort has already been spent. Huge changes like that would not normally be allowed. Governments move slower than snails, especially here in Germany where a consensus is needed for the smallest detail… Um, I must think." She paced about the room deep in thought. "One cannot simply stop a project because of the whim of an elf, or a Minister of Transportation, for that matter. There is nothing environmentally precious there, all tests have been done…" she continued mumbling.

Penelope was listening and a spark ignited in her thoughts. She spoke aloud, "I once had to do a report on archaeology and there was this excavation site in Italy where they discovered old bones or something and it was right where they were building a new supermarket. And they had to stop building the new store, even though it was almost finished and…"

"Construction had to be halted and dismantled, for fear of destroying ancient artifacts. That's it, child. You have solved the problem."

Digging for Clues

"What has she done? Discovered dinosaur bones or something?" interrupted a bewildered Amelia.

Frau Glauberin spoke at once, "She's done it. Amelia, if something special and very old, old enough to belong to a… an extinct species or long forgotten ancestor of ours, is found in the soil around the rail-line site, all further construction has to stop. This is because there may be other interesting and important objects to be found. All these objects can tell us more about the lifestyles and scientific advancements of the ancient society. In this case, it is the undiscovered society of the elves. It is very helpful to our own race to learn about other peoples who lived on this same land…" She would have continued but Schönelieberin, who was taking sharp intakes of breath, interrupted her.

"Other peoples, our own race? What are you saying? Are you completely human now, dear Regenbogen? Do you not feel like an elf?" She bowed her lovely head. "Are you not my sister?"

Penelope saw that Frau Glauberin looked at her elfin sister with a warm and soft expression. She, herself, felt as if she knew how to answer. So she did.

"Yes, Schönelieberin, she is and will always be your sister. Just because she is human now doesn't mean she can't love you and feel in her heart that you two are blood-related. Once you have a sister, you always do." She squinted her eyes and peered at Amelia, who was grinning and rolling her eyes. "Besides, the two of you are proof that humans and elves can get along."

"Hear, hear!" clapped and cheered the others. Mondwagen stopped his sobbing long enough to mutter, "Yes, but now our sacred land will be crawling with scientists and other nosy humans. How will we live under their feet? Oh my, oh my, I prefer extinction by train."

"Nonsense, friend Mondwagen," boomed out the deep voice of Himmelwort, whose height and girth seemed quite impressive now with Frau Glauberin at his side. "We can leave all sorts of things for the scientists to find. And we can place them where we want the humans to look. We will keep it to a certain area...like Stonehenge in England. The humans don't have a clue about THAT! And it takes up only a small bit of land." He cupped his chin in his hand. "Now let's see, what outfit can I part with that will both tempt and satisfy the researchers? It will have to be museum-quality," he said with a serious expression and a twinkle in his eye.

"Yes and..." Frau Glauberin looked at Himmelwort and batted her eyelashes, "the ICE rail line can be rerouted around your specific area. That is physically and financially, not to mention, politically possible."

Penelope clapped her hands and looked around the office at the scene. Amelia was dancing about with Schönelieberin. Himmelwort and Frau Glauberin were holding hands and whispering. Mondwagen was drying his tears with a dripping handkerchief, and Hoch was talking intently with of all people, Penelope's mother. Curious as to what they were discussing she headed their way.

Hoch saw her coming and turned toward Penelope and bowed. He smiled as he said "We have much to be grateful and most thankful for, dear child. You have proven your worth to the entire elfin community. He turned and she saw him wink at her mother. "We wish to bestow upon you a great honor. Hence forth, you will be known as Penelope, Esteemed Daughter of the Elves."

Penelope was about to respond when her mother broke in, "Penelope, I had no idea this was...going on." She made a motion with her hand taking in all the elves. "I am still in shock. How silly we must have seemed? Oh my gosh, Mrs....I mean, Frau Doctor Kopffall? What shall I say to her?"

Amelia came skipping over to Penelope's aid. "Just tell the Doctor she'd better get her head checked."

Everyone laughed until a knock at the office door silenced the merriment. Frau Glauberin walked to the door and opened it a small way.

"Yes, can I help you, Frau Steinaugen?"

"Ach, Jah. I heard it vas a bit loud in *dere. Vat wid* only *zwei Kinder* and a *Mutter* it seemed impossible. Is *everysing* okay, Frau Glauberin?" Frau Steinaugen craned her chicken-like neck and tried to peer inside the room to satisfy her curiosity.

"Jah, natürlich. Alles ist in Ordnung, Frau Steinaugen. Danke."[107] Frau Glauberin gently closed the door behind her and winked

---

[107]Yes, naturally. All is in order, Mrs. Steinaugen. (Stone-eyes) Thank you

at her friends. "I don't think Frau Steinaugen is ready for elves just yet."

Penelope agreed with a nod and a laugh. But this did give her an idea. Most people were a bit like the secretary. After they grasped the fact that elves once existed, seeing the artifacts and all, people would still resist believing that elves were alive today, she reckoned. Maybe she could find a way to ease them into it. She looked over at the long beard and stern face of Hoch and …that was it. She had it. COMPUTERS!

She startled herself as she didn't realize that she had said this last word out loud. Everyone was looking at her expecting an explanation.

"Oh, I was just thinking to myself about how to explain elves to people who just won't believe it…and I thought we might try using a website or something where they could visit and learn and ask questions and…"

"Email! People could email the elves and talk to them and that would help them believe," exclaimed Amelia in a rush. "What a cool idea."

Penelope glanced over at Hoch. She knew he hated all technological things about humans, especially their fascination and reliance on computers. 'Well he will just have to learn,' she decided and gave her hair a serious twist.

Himmelwort was all for the idea. "You mean people could ask me questions, like fashion do's and don'ts? I love it. Or better, I could advise them on elf-etiquette and such…What to wear to an elf wedding. He winked at Frau Glauberin who turned a shade brighter than her *Dirndl*.[108]

---

[108]Traditional peasant costume, a dress with an apron, worn mostly in Southern Germany and Austria

Even Mondwagen piped in "Could I access the stock exchange?"

Hoch gave him a dark look and held up his hand. "All matters will be discussed at our sacred meeting place in the forest we hold dear. All those who have helped our cause shall attend and be recognized." He turned to Penelope and spoke. "My child, it seems in aiding us you are changing us. However, I believe it is for our good. It is time for us to adapt once more. He smiled, "Even if we must become 'elvesonline.com'."

Full Circle in the Wood

As the three Pond children made their way through the woods, Penelope noticed the ground was softer under her feet and was covered with a carpet of tiny white flowers.[109] It made the dark woods brighten and appear lit from below. She remembered how nervous she was the first time she entered these woods and smiled to herself as she pondered how much had changed. To think that once all she worried about was her silly height. Now she couldn't wait to show her little brother the magical place she knew and loved.

The trio entered the sacred circle of stones, each stone supporting an elf as before. This time, however, the circle had grown. Liedersinger was not there, but rather the beautiful, glowing, Schönelieberin. Seated next to her was Frau Glauberin, who looked quite at home in a bright orange Dirndl, her shiny locket glistening in a sunbeam.

To the right of Frau Glauberin, was an amazing sight. Himmelwort was a burst of color. He was covered mostly in a shimmering purple robe, with a bright orange sash. At his side was a long silver sword with a ruby hilt. The hand, which rested on the hilt, was adorned with many jeweled rings. On his

---

[109]Wood Anemone-flowers Mar-May

face was the biggest grin Penelope had ever seen. She looked to Hoch for an explanation.

"Greetings, Penelope, Esteemed Daughter of the Elves," His gaze fell on Amelia, "and most Ambitious Amelia, Champion of the Elves." To Tucker, he rose and bowed before the small boy. "I thank you, little one, for your understanding and your never-failing aid. I name thee, *Taschentuch*,[110] Helper of the Elves." Hoch motioned for the children to find a stone and be seated. "Taschentuch," he explained, "believes in elves and has always been able to see and hear us elves just as every other child age five years or younger. All very young children have open and free hearts, a freedom that diminishes, sadly, with age." He looked over at Penelope and Amelia and smiled. "Fortunately, this unquestioning openness is replaced by wisdom and a conscience.

"Taschentuch, what does that mean?" whispered Amelia to Penelope. "And why didn't Tucker tell us he knew about the elves all along? He could have saved us a lot of trouble!" Amelia rolled her eyes and held up her hands. "Hoch called me 'Am-bi-shus' Amelia. Is that good or bad?"

"Tucker's means handkerchief. Probably because he always has a runny nose! Still, it sounds sweet, doesn't it?" answered Penelope as she cocked her head to one side. She turned back to her sister. "And yes, Tucker told me he saw Hoch many times. You just never listened. Ambitious is good, silly. I think it means you like new things." She put her finger to her lips and pointed at Hoch, now standing in the center of the ring. He announced,

---

[110]Handkerchief

119

"I have called you all here to our sacred circle in the wood for a special meeting and to share in an honored celebration. As you are all aware, because of the persistence and faith of dear friend, Penelope, and her comrades," he nodded in their direction; "the elfin people have been spared." The Elfin Prophecy is soon fulfilled. As we sit here, elfin artifacts have been placed around this area of the ICE-line, waiting to be 'discovered'. Work on the rail line has been stopped momentarily due to the need of a new construction site chief." Hoch cleared his throat, and turned his stare on Frau Glauberin and Himmelwort.

"As for Frau Glauberin, I have been informed that she wishes henceforth in our presence to be addressed as Regenbogen. And I have also been informed," Hoch paused for effect, "that she and elf friend, Himmelwort wish to be married."

A loud cheer rose from the stones. All were on their feet congratulating the colorful pair. Hoch let the merriment continue for a bit and then raised his hand in the familiar silencing gesture. The noise quieted as everyone sat back down and waited.

"My last announcement might come as a shock to most of you. It was to me." He looked over at Mondwagen who was already getting to his feet. "It seems that it *is* possible for Regenbogen to become an elf once more." Again, everyone started talking and gesturing. "Elf professor, Mondwagen, will explain."

Mondwagen stood in the center and slipped on a pair of blue rimmed glasses. He unrolled a yellowed scroll like the one the Prophecy was written on and read from the old parchment.

The Protection Charm binds the elf
Forever to embody another.
Power to retransform alas,
Can only be found at the rainbow's end

Hoch finished reading and looked at everyone over his glasses. He turned and faced Himmelwort and Regenbogen. "We must wait for the appearance of a rainbow, elf friends. Only then may the two of you marry as elves and live long elfin lives together."

Penelope could not resist asking, "But why can't they get married now? They love each other. Why does Frau Glauberin, I mean Regenbogen, have to be an elf?"

Mondwagen peered over his glasses at her. "Because my dear child, Himmelwort the *elf*, he emphasized this word, "will live at least until he is three hundred earth years old, and Frau Glauberin here, well, she will not live as long." Embarrassed, Mondwagen sat back down in a rush.

"But what about the rail line? Who will make sure it is re-routed if Frau Glaub...I mean Regenbogen is not there?" asked Penelope twisting her hair.

It was Regenbogen's turn to stand up and address the ring. "Don't worry. Frau Glauberin's work is done. The pieces are already in place as Hoch described. The next step comes when a human discovers the artfully hidden elfin artifacts. The rail line will be re-routed, I assure you." She paused for a moment and then added, "I have another announcement to make."

She looked with twinkling eyes at Himmelwort, "We have discussed and decided together that we wish to start our lives anew and make our home in my old home. That is, we want to move back to the rainforest, the land of my birth. Together we will rebuild the elfin community. It is my duty and my wish to carry out the vision that was Regenbogen, daughter of the rainbow." She looked at Penelope and her brother and sister, and then in turn, gazed at the elves. She stopped at Schönelieberin, who was crying tears of joy. The sisters hugged each other. "I believe we can make magic, once more, in the rain forest."

"I, too, wish to return to the rainforest. May I join you dear sister?" Everyone already knew the answer.

Himmelwort stood up and Penelope could tell he was bursting with happiness. "I just wanted to say that those pesky Leprechauns were right. There is a pot of gold at the end of the rainbow!" Everyone clapped and cheered even louder when he added with an impish grin, "Tell me, what do the fashion magazines say they are wearing now, in the rain forests?"

Pot of Gold

An excited Penelope ran home from the bus stop, trying to avoid the raindrops and dodging the puddles of the very wet spring season. Amelia and Tucker lagged behind. By the time the two caught up, she had an idea.

"Hey, let's go down to the post office and get some candy? Mommy's not home yet. She probably had another appointment with Frau Doctor Kopffall." Amelia and Tucker, who they now called Taschentuch, nodded with knowing expressions.

The three Pond children raced down the wet, glistening, narrow streets to their favorite shop. Inside Penelope studied the assorted candies as Amelia pondered over the horseback riding magazines. Tucker grabbed a handful of *sauer gummis* and placed them on the counter. Penelope added her stockpile and looked into the reddening face of the post lady. The woman looked ready to burst. However, she didn't scream at them but rather spoke to a woman in line behind them. Penelope understood what she was saying in German,

"*Ja*[111], my son has a new job. Klausi has been transferred to an oilrig. It is good-paying but it is very cold, right near

---

[111] Yes

the North Pole." She then glared at the trio as she tallied their purchases. She looked very unhappy.

Penelope stifled a laugh and coughed instead. Hexe looked up and pointed at Penelope, *"Es ist deine Fehle!"*[112] Amelia gasped out loud. Penelope turned to her sister, and saw that Amelia was looking at something else. Her face was white and she was holding a newspaper in her hand. Penelope glanced at the headline, **Seltsamer Fund an Eisenbahn Baustelle!**[113] The German was too difficult to understand, but the photograph underneath told the story.

There, in black and white, was the ICE rail line construction site with a man standing, holding a long, silver sword. One could barely make out the jeweled handle. Himmelwort's sword! She looked at an open-mouthed Amelia. The first sign of the elves...Hurray! They dropped a handful of coins onto the counter and ran out of the post office before anyone could say *Auf Wiedersehen.*

As they waited for a slower Taschentuch to catch up, Penelope and Amelia speculated as to what the German papers might be saying about the newly 'found' sword. "I hope it says they're stopping construction right away," panted Amelia.

"I'm sure they don't want to destroy important stuff," agreed Penelope as she scanned the article looking for words she knew. The girls continued reading and guessing and did not notice the crowd in front of the *Bäckerei*. Amelia bumped into a stout, older woman with a jolt.

"Es tut mir leid[114]," she apologized in a small, embarrassed voice. But the woman barely gave her a glance. She was too

---

[112]"It's your fault!"
[113]Strange Discovery at the Railway Construction Site!
[114]I'm sorry.

busy talking to the other adults, who were waving their arms, smiling and nodding to one another.

Penelope perked up and tried to follow the conversation. It had to be big news, she reckoned, because she had never seen more than a half dozen people out in the village at one time. Then she heard it...*"Ja, unglaublich! Es gibt Elfen hier in Deutschland!"*[115]

They were talking about the elves, her elves. People were starting to believe. She turned to Amelia, who she could see, had also understood the German. Penelope grabbed her by both arms and the two did a merry jig right in the middle of the street. After a couple of happy turns, Penelope realized that Tucker hadn't caught up yet.

"Taschentuch, where are you?" she yelled behind them. "Come, catch up."

They waited until his small shape appeared from around the last bend. Oddly, he was walking backwards and shuffling along. The girls saw that he was looking and pointing at something far away. Then, they saw it too.

A rainbow, a huge multi-colored arching and stretching rainbow! The colors were the brightest Penelope had ever seen. The purple stripe matched the robe Himmelwort wore. He really did have good taste, she thought with a smile. She would miss him a lot when he moved to the rainforest. But, she remembered that they would keep in touch via emails in the future. The elves sure caught on fast to human advances in technology. And Hoch himself designed the website. She shook her head, 'my how things have changed.'

---

[115] Yes, unbelievable! There are elves here in Germany!

Lost in thought, she was lulled back to the present by a hushed, but awe-inspired hum from the crowd in front of the *Bäckerei*. They, too, had noticed the spectacular rainbow. Still mesmerized she realized Taschentuch was talking to her.

"Can you see them, Peppy? Are they married yet?"

Oh-ma-gosh! He was right. This must be the one. She and Amelia strained their eyes to see the wedding couple. But all that they could see was a fading haze of colors.

Penelope didn't need to see. She knew in her heart what lay at the end of the rainbow...ELVES.

The Big Announcement

Smiling and feeling quite proud of themselves, the three skipped home, never once groaning about the *Altstadt's* steep climbing streets. In the house, Penelope scaled the spiral staircase slowly, stopping on each step to think about the entire adventure. Downstairs, she heard the basement door slam, and knew that her dad had just come home from work. 'Boy, he is in for a major surprise,' she laughed to herself.

"I'm home, everyone," she heard the familiar greeting. Then he yelled, "Guess what? I have some interesting news for all of you."

Grinning and shaking her head she started back down the stairs knowing full well what her dad was going to say. He must have seen the headlines. Finally, he understands her 'elf-problem' and is ready to apologize and congratulate her. Maybe he even brought her a present? She decided Amelia and Tucker too should be present.

"Hey everyone, Daddy is home! He has some…umm… important news for us." Penelope yelled trying not to let her satisfaction sound in her voice.

Mr. Pond motioned for the family to be seated in the small, darkened living area. Mrs. Pond joined them after hanging up the phone. Penelope watched her dad and twisted her hair into ringlets. She could barely keep still. It wasn't the first time she wanted to scream out…ELVES I TOLD YOU SO! She was looking forward to school and rubbing in it to all the kids in her class. A great summer of sweet revenge lay ahead. But she managed to remain silent and wore only a huge grin.

"So, as I was saying. This is so exciting," she listened to her dad exclaim. "You all have been so understanding and I am so proud of you, especially Penelope, Amelia and Tucker." He looked in her direction and winked. At that moment she wanted to stand up and shout, "I know! I told you there were elves here…" But before her legs could move an inch, her dad spoke up.

"Germany has been such an adventure for our entire family, and I think we have all enjoyed living here. It took some getting used to, I realize," he glanced at Penelope, who clapped and nodded in agreement. Mr. Pond raised his brows a little but continued, "The weather could have been sunnier, and the stores open longer," he chuckled and looked at Mrs. Pond, who sat saying nothing, on the sofa. "I will certainly miss the *Biergartens*,"[116] he winked. "We all learned to speak German, well…" Mr. Pond hung his head, "at least the four of you did, I tried but…but what a wonderful time we have had here. The German people have been very welcoming. We have made many good friends. The food, well…" he patted his rounded stomach and smiled, "the food is way too delicious and…"

Penelope began to suspect something was wrong. Things were not moving in the direction of elves fast enough. She

---

[116]Translates as Beer Garden, a restaurant with outdoor seating serving traditional German fare

decided to speed up the announcement. She jumped to her feet and cried out, "Okay, Dad. We all know you're just trying to make us wait. Everyone already knows...because of the news and the newspapers and even Frau Breymann, the PIANO TEACHER, knows."

She was not prepared for his reply.

"How do they know we are moving to England if I haven't even told you, my family, yet?"

School Day Challenge

Everything was winding down the last week of school. Penelope felt both happy and sad, as she, Amelia, and Tucker boarded the bus for nearly the last ride to the International School. She would miss her new found friends in Germany, *human and elf,* she smiled to herself. After the news of elves existing in Germany had made the headlines worldwide, Penelope had been enjoying her secret success, even if only the elves and she and her family, well, except her Dad, knew the whole story. The media had given her, Penelope Pond, the credit for stopping the ICE train line from destroying ancient artifacts. Everyone at school had been so surprised and proud of her. And although no one yet had actually seen an elf, people wanted to believe that elves actually existed once upon a time. People were at least talking about elfin populations in times past. The internet blogs and website were a start, and were creating more interest in elves. The best part was the new respect she had from Herr Von Lehmden. Now when he screamed at her during her riding lessons, he followed it with a wink.

"Still," she sighed, "I wish I could make everyone see that the elves are more than 'old bones'. They are ALIVE!"

Amelia elbowed Penelope in her ribs, "Who is alive? Who are you talking to? I don't see any elves on the bus." Amelia turned and checked out the passengers.

"Oh Amelia, I'm just wishing my class could meet the elves...in person! If I could make just one friend see an elf?" Penelope tugged her hair and looked out the window as they pulled into the school parking lot. The large modern school was busy with parents dropping off children and students walking into the building. Suddenly she shouted with glee! "Look! Amelia! Tucker! Over there! There are the elves...what are they doing? What is Himmelwort wearing?" She began waving and pointing toward the glass doors of the school. "They must have come to say goodbye before we move to England."

Indeed, an odd sight greeted Penelope and she walked up to the entrance. Hoch and the elves were standing in a row like students lined up for class. Each elf carried a back-pack and a lunch box except Himmelwort, who pulled a suitcase on wheels. Penelope noted that he was wearing *Lederhosen*,[117] the traditional German outfit of short pants with suspenders made from leather. He looked like he was going to yodel at any moment. Penelope ran up to the elves.

"Hoch, Himmelwort! What are you doing here? You look... well like kids!"

"What does it look like we're doing my dear?" answered Himmelwort looking down his nose at Penelope. "We are going to school." He pointed to his Lederhosen, "I haven't worn these since I was a young elf in *Gymnasium*."[118]

---

[117]Traditional Bavarian trousers made of leather. Bavaria is a large state, located in the south of Germany.
[118]Gymnasium is a German academic high school

131

Hoch added, nodding to the others, "It appears you were quite a bit thinner back then, Himmelwort. I advise that you don't sit down today. It may prove embarrassing."

"Nonsense, I am as fit as ever." Himmelwort smiled at the Pond children, patting his bulging belly, "And please tell me, when is lunch served? I am starved just thinking about schoolwork."

Penelope smiled and shook her head. "Well, I guess we can split you up and each of you can come to class with one of us." She looked left and right to Amelia and Tucker.

Mondwagen, who had been standing silently and sulking spoke up, "If I must go to school, I would prefer to join Tucker in Kindergarten. I like to color, you know."

Amelia piped up, "Where is Regenbogen? You guys are married now, aren't you Himmelwort? We saw the rainbow."

"My dear wife, my most beautiful companion, is busy packing for our journey to the Rain Forest." Himmelwort turned bright red and stammered, "She...ummm...asked me to leave and get out...she asked me to do something useful while she packs. Therefore I am helping you!" he stuttered and pointed directly at Amelia with a lop-sided grin.

Amelia tilted her curly head and shrugged her shoulders saying, "Okay then Himmelwort, you are coming with me to Ms. Wrobleski's class. She is a very strict teacher and we are learning fractions and stuff. I'll have to help you," she stated matter-of-factly and began walking into school.

Hoch and Penelope were left standing alone. As if reading her thoughts, Hoch said "Perhaps we can convince one of your friends today that elves walk among you. I bow to you, dear Penelope to provide the person and the passion to change him or her. One boy or girl will make a big..." his words trailed off.

Penelope had an idea. Quickly she smiled and grabbed Hoch's arm. "I know just the boy we are going to sit next to in German class." She led Hoch across the large gathering room with a high ceiling made of shiny wood and huge beams crossing overhead. They continued down a carpeted hall into a bright large classroom. Windows lined the wall framing a view of farmers' fields and open meadows.

Penelope spied Marcus sitting in the last row and winked at Hoch, who sat down next to Marcus placing his backpack in the aisle between the desks. Penelope flopped down at the desk in front of Marcus, who immediately said, "Oh, it's the elf-girl? See any elves today?" and placed his fingers over his head making the shape of pointy ears.

To Marcus' dismay, Penelope laughed and said, "If you only knew you are sitting right next to the leader of the elves, right now!" and she pointed at where Hoch was sitting.

Marcus looked a little worried as he glanced over at the empty chair. He looked back at Penelope with a sneer. "You are crazy. My parents even said so. They talked to my Aunt who is a *Schul-psychologe*[119] and she said your whole family is crazy..."

"You mean your Aunt is...Frau Doctor Kopffall?" Penelope was aghast, but then she changed her tone and said with authority. "Actually, your Aunt is wrong and so are you! I am here to prove to you once and for all...the elves are *real*. I can tell Marcus that you are afraid! You are afraid to believe in

---

[119]Educational Psychologist

elves! Scare-dy cat!" She turned around and faced the front of the room, knowing Marcus couldn't resist the challenge.

"I am NOT AFRAID. I could believe if I wanted, so there." Marcus replied in anger.

"Oh Yeah? So prove it! Look at Hoch, the elf here, and try to believe in him. Think about it real hard. You can get mad at him too if you want, unless you're CHICKEN!" Penelope taunted.

"Okay, where is this elf?" Marcus turned and focused on the desk beside him. "I am going to show him a thing or two…" After a full minute or two Marcus stood up and declared he couldn't see anyone. He tried to walk away when he suddenly tripped in the aisle and landed face down on his stomach. "Hey, who put this here?"

Penelope couldn't believe it. Marcus was pointing to Hoch's backpack! Marcus could see and feel it! She picked up the backpack and held it up in front of Marcus' face. "This is THE ELF'S backpack!" She looked over at Hoch who was motioning to her to open the backpack. "Let's just see what an elf packs inside?" she mumbled and held it open for Marcus to see.

Penelope had his attention alright. Marcus paused and looked into the backpack. He picked out a small stone. As he was examining it, Hoch spoke, "What do you expect to see in there, fairy dust?"

"No, I thought maybe something magical, not just a rock… Whoa…Wait a minute. Who's talking?" With these trembling words Marcus looked up and over at the desk. A ray of sun beamed in through the windows and shown directly upon Hoch. He appeared to glow.

"What? Who? Ohmagosh! Are you...? You are...the ELF?!! Help!" Marcus, overcome with shock and discovery, and a little afraid, ran out of the room screaming for the teacher.

Penelope and Hoch both burst out laughing. "We sure showed him." Penelope laughed until tears came out. "I hope he goes running to his dear Aunt Frau Doctor Kopffall!" She and Hoch laughed louder as each pictured the doubting counselor's surprise at her own nephew's 'elfin delusion.' When Penelope could stop laughing she said to Hoch in all seriousness, "So, do you think this is enough? Is one more boy who knows and believes enough to convince everyone else?"

"Patience. We elves can wait for one doubting Marcus at a time. His word will go a long way. One year ago we had no believers. Today, thanks to you Penelope, we have believers, and more significant is now our sacred forest is safe from destruction. Tomorrow we Wood Elves will live once more in harmony with the human race." Hoch mumbled further, "Can't say the same about our distant friends, the Leprechauns. In fact, when you arrive in England..."

Penelope wanted to ask him what he was talking about when a loud bell rang in the building, and all the students pulled out their notebooks as Frau Huybrechts entered the room. She looked around the room until she saw Penelope and said aloud, "Whatever did you say to Marcus? The boy looks like he's seen a ghost!" She put on her glasses saying, "Today we are reading the fairytales of the Brothers' Grimm in their original German language."

Hoch jumped out of his seat and prepared to leave the classroom. To Penelope's surprise, he clasped her hand in his and whispered, "I bid you farewell, brave Penelope. The elves will always remain at your service." He nodded toward the teacher, who was reading aloud in German the story of <u>Rumpelstiltskin,</u> and said with a wink, "I remember Jacob and Willie Grimm. They were nice boys who got along well with the elves! I'm glad to hear they shared their adventures with the rest of you. Fairy Tales, indeed!" With that, Hoch, the elf, vanished.

A Giant Beginning

Penelope unbuckled her seat belt as the plane taxied to a stop at the gate. Trying to keep up with the hurried pace of all the other passengers, she and her family grabbed their carry-on luggage and pulled them down the narrow aisle of the British Airway's Airbus.

Trudging through the huge terminal at London's Heathrow Airport, Penelope's eager eyes scanned the area. The signs were easy to read. They were all in English. The travelers were not as tall as Germans she noted, although everyone here also loved to dress in dark colors. It was also raining outside. That was nothing new. It was only one year ago since she first saw Himmelwort, dressed as a ballet dancer, in the Frankfurt airport. Wow, so much had changed. Lost in thought, she didn't notice that Amelia had stopped the luggage cart, brimming with Beanie Babies and backpacks, and Penelope banged right into it.

"Ouch. Amelia, what are you doing?"

"These English luggage carts are just like Germany's. My friend Rachel from England said their luggage carts were the best, but these wheels are dumb too; they all wiggle and...," she rolled her eyes, and then she stopped mid sentence. "Whoa, that man is so tall," Amelia pointed with her mouth hanging open.

Penelope followed the direction of Amelia's finger until she saw what Amelia was seeing. She turned with wide eyes and whispered to Amelia, "He must be a giant."

"Girls, behave yourselves. Stop pointing," Mrs. Pond whispered without making her lips move. "It is not polite to stare…or point for that matter," she added with a frown. Then Mrs. Pond noticed what had gotten the girls attention. She stuttered, "Oh my, he IS a tall fellow."

"Pick me up, Mommy. I want to see too," whined Tucker who couldn't see over the many heads in the terminal.

"Here you go son." Mr. Pond swung Tucker up onto his shoulders and they both turned toward the extremely tall man who was standing about 10 meters away.[120] The stranger had his back to them. Suddenly he turned around as if he felt their gaze and looked over all the heads of the crowded terminal until his eyes found the Pond Family.

"Mom…Dad. Don't look now but…he's staring at us!" Penelope could barely get the words out she was so astonished. "Ohmagosh! He's walking towards us…"

"I told you not to be rude. This is so embarrsing." Mrs. Pond shook her head and her hands. She glanced at her husband. "Ben, let's just apologize and be on our way…"

As the very tall stranger approached, many heads in the airport turned to watch. Penelope could see that she and her family weren't the only ones who thought the man was odd. "Why is he coming over to us?" she wondered as she grabbed

---

[120] A little more than 32 feet as a meter measures 39.37 inches, a little longer than a yard.

a few strands of hair and began to twist. To her great surprise and now a nagging fear, the man adjusted his gaze and focused straight on her alone.

"Penelope, he's coming to get YOU!" Amelia too had noticed his shift in gaze. She looked at Penelope with liquid brown worry in her eyes. "Ugh uh! He looks angry. And he's carrying a big stick," Amelia raised her brows and quietly slid behind Mrs. Pond, peering from behind her mom at her helpless sister.

The room darkened as the very tall man stood over the huddled Pond family. All five of them looked up into his face, including Tucker who was still enjoying his perch on Mr. Pond's shoulders. Penelope stood quite still as she bent her head completely back and looked straight up into the stranger's eyes. "My they are a pretty shade of green," was her first thought.

As if reading her mind, the imposing stranger said in a dancing voice that was as low and deep as the lowest note on the piano keyboard, "Green as green greetins' I bring ye. Top a' da' morning to ya', miss. Zachary O'Cornwell at your service and your guide throughout our lovely lands." In welcome he extended his huge hand.

Penelope let go of her knotted hair and held out her small hand. It was immediately engulfed inside the stranger's grip. She looked questioningly over at her parents who both stood stunned into silence. It was obvious they had no idea what to expect either. 'Guess it's up to me as usual to figure these strange things out,' she finally reckoned. 'It can't be stranger than elves!' she smiled to herself.

"Oh you see there. There's the gleam I was a lookin' for miss. Hoch, the lad, informed me you'd come 'round quick as a jackrabbit." He released his hold on Penelope and smoothed his long brown pants with his iron-like hands. "If ye all would just follow me, I'll have you through customs with all that baggage, and well on your merry way…" He stopped and appeared to notice Tucker for the first time sitting high on Mr. Pond. The very tall Mr. O'Cornwell still had to look *down* to speak to the boy. "What a fine lad ye be boy, and a fine five at that. Let's go see about collectin' your cat." With these words he raised his hand in a high five salute which Tucker immediately responded with a slap of his own. Penelope's daze and wonderment was shattered when Amelia spoke up.

"Why should we go with you? Who are you?" Amelia stated with hands on her hips. She looked and nodded to her dad for backup.

"Why? To see our thriving Leprechaun colony just north of London town, little miss. Hoch gave yours truly," Mr. O'Cornwell raised his cane, "specific instructions to take care of ye. And you know it's not wise to make Mr. Hoch cross. So, let's step lively and…"

Mr. Pond shook his head briefly as if to wake himself from a dream. He cleared his throat. Penelope could tell he was putting on his 'Dad' face, the one where he was the boss. Did he hear the man say Leprechaun? She was still not sure if her dad was ever convinced about the existence of elves. He never actually said he believed her.

In fact, her dad had never said anything other than he was happy that she was happy at school, and was proud Penelope had made such a difference in re-routing the ICE line. He had apologized for their sudden move to England, but he was always so serious about his job.

What *was* he going to say to this very odd, complete stranger, who was talking about Leprechauns? Mr. O'Cornwell was a *Leprechaun?!* He is way too tall. It was too much, too strange. Dad is going to blow his top, she concluded. She looked at her dad's reddening face and waited.

Before her father could respond to the stranger, Mrs. Pond interrupted, "Now Ben, I realize you thought the elf-thing was a bit strange and unbelievable but I swear it was real. Let's give this nice man…umm Leprechaun, a chance." She cast her eyes over to the doubting Amelia. "Honey, he said he knows Hoch. That is proof enough for me."

Amelia looked at her mom in amazement. "Wow, Mom. You are so cool." She turned back to her dad and said in a reassuring grownup tone, "Its okay Dad. He knows Hoch. You know, the ELF?" and she made her hands stroke an imaginary beard.

Penelope turned and looked upwards at the grinning Mr. O'Cornwell and then in turn at her dad who, despite her height, was still at least a head taller than she. She saw him nod to the stranger who immediately leaned over to allow Tucker to climb onto his tall shoulders. Tucker scrambled up onto the giant man's broad shoulders. Amelia placed her small hand into the stranger's large one, and she and the giant, on whom Tucker perched like an eagle, walked away accompanied by a chatty Mrs. Pond who was explaining her in-depth knowledge about elves and such.

Penelope and her father remained behind, and coolly scanned the situation. She looked up to her dad once again.

He smiled suddenly, showing all his teeth, and cupping her chin tenderly in his palm, asked, "Penelope, my dear little hero, are there elves in England *as well?*"

Penelope answered him with a giant hug. "I don't know, Dad," she sighed happily. "Hoch said the only magic creatures left in the UK were Leprechauns, and that they were mostly in Ireland." She observed her father's face closely for signs of teasing, but saw his expression was beaming with pride. So when he tilted his head in the direction of the other family members already engaged in animated conversation with the very tall Mr. O'Cornwell and said, "Shall we join them?"

She didn't hesitate. Ready for another adventure in a foreign land, Penelope stood tall and skipped toward the sign marked "WAY OUT."

Breinigsville, PA USA
08 October 2009
225449BV00001B/4/P